Drawn
- by a -
China Moon

Trailblazer Books

Gladys Aylward ▪ *Flight of the Fugitives*
Mary McLeod Bethune ▪ *Defeat of the Ghost Riders*
William & Catherine Booth ▪ *Kidnapped by River Rats*
Governor William Bradford ▪ *The Mayflower Secret*
John Bunyan ▪ *Traitor in the Tower*
Amy Carmichael ▪ *The Hidden Jewel**
Peter Cartwright ▪ *Abandoned on the Wild Frontier*
George Washington Carver ▪ *The Forty-Acre Swindle*
Elizabeth Fry ▪ *The Thieves of Tyburn Square*
Jonathan & Rosalind Goforth ▪ *Mask of the Wolf Boy*
Barbrooke Grubb ▪ *Ambushed in Jaguar Swamp*
Sheldon Jackson ▪ *The Gold Miners' Rescue*
Adoniram & Ann Judson ▪ *Imprisoned in the Golden City*
Festo Kivengere ▪ *Assassins in the Cathedral*
David Livingstone ▪ *Escape From the Slave Traders**
Martin Luther ▪ *Spy for the Night Riders**
Dwight L. Moody ▪ *Danger on the Flying Trapeze*
Lottie Moon ▪ *Drawn by a China Moon*
Samuel Morris ▪ *Quest for the Lost Prince*
George Müller ▪ *The Bandit of Ashley Downs*
John Newton ▪ *The Runaway's Revenge*
Florence Nightingale ▪ *The Drummer Boy's Battle*
William Penn ▪ *Hostage on the Nighthawk*
Joy Ridderhof ▪ *Race for the Record*
Nate Saint ▪ *The Fate of the Yellow Woodbee*
William Seymour ▪ *Journey to the End of the Earth*
Menno Simons ▪ *The Betrayer's Fortune*
Mary Slessor ▪ *Trial by Poison*
Hudson Taylor ▪ *Shanghaied to China**
Harriet Tubman ▪ *Listen for the Whippoorwill*
William Tyndale ▪ *The Queen's Smuggler*
John Wesley ▪ *The Chimney Sweep's Ransom*
Marcus & Narcissa Whitman ▪ *Attack in the Rye Grass*
David Zeisberger ▪ *The Warrior's Challenge*

Also by Dave and Neta Jackson

Hero Tales: A Family Treasury of True Stories
From the Lives of Christian Heroes (Volumes I, II, & III)

*Curriculum guide available.
Written by Julia Pferdehirt with Dave & Neta Jackson.   00C

Drawn
– by a –
China Moon

Dave & Neta Jackson

Illustrated by Anne Gavitt

BETHANY HOUSE PUBLISHERS
MINNEAPOLIS, MINNESOTA 55438

Published by Bethany House Publishers
A Ministry of Bethany Fellowship International
11400 Hampshire Avenue South
Minneapolis, Minnesota 55438
www.bethanyhouse.com

Printed in the United States of America by
Bethany Press International, Minneapolis, Minnesota 55438

Library of Congress Cataloging-in-Publication Data

Jackson, Dave.
    Drawn by a China moon : Lottie Moon / by Dave & Neta Jackson ; story illustrations by Anne Gavitt.
       p. cm. — (Trailblazer books)
    Summary: When her best friend Ida moves to China with her missionary parents in the late 1800s, Mollie receives letters from her, including tales of Lottie Moon, a groundbreaking female missionary.
      ISBN 0–7642–2267–8 (pbk.)
    [1. Moon, Lottie, 1840–1912—Fiction. 2. Pen pals—Fiction.
3. Best friends—Fiction. 4. Friendship—Fiction. 5. Missionaries—Fiction. 6. Christian life—Fiction. 7. China—History—1861–1912—Fiction.] I. Jackson, Neta. II. Gavitt, Anne, ill. III. Title.
PZ7.J132418 Do 2000
[Fic] dc21
                                                 00–010471

This story basically follows the events in Lottie Moon's life between 1893 during her first furlough home to Virginia—after twenty years in China—to the end of the Boxer Rebellion in China in 1901.

We chose to tell Lottie Moon's story through the eyes of two fictional American friends—one a missionary's daughter in China, and the other a typical girl in turn-of-the-century Virginia. This approach shows the very real sacrifices of men, women, and children who left home, family, and friends to answer God's call to take the Gospel to other countries, especially before modern means of travel and communication.

The character of Mollie Jones is loosely based on the real-life story of Jessie Pettigrew, a member of her mother's Sunbeam Band in a Southern Baptist church, who at the age of fifteen or sixteen met Lottie Moon sometime during her first furlough (1891–1893). Jessie later became a nurse and went to China as a missionary in 1901 at the age of twenty-four to help meet the desperate need for medical personnel.

Ida Baker, however, is totally fictional.

Find us on the Web at . . .

Trailblazerbooks.com

- Meet the authors.

- Read the first chapter of each book—
  with the pictures.

- Track the Trailblazers around the world
  on a map.

- Use the historical timeline to find out
  what other important events were happening in the world at the time of each
  Trailblazer story.

- Discover how the authors research their
  books and link to some of the same
  sources they used where
  you can learn more
  about these heroes.

- Write to the authors.

- Explore frequently asked
  questions about writing
  and Trailblazer books.

> **LIMITED OFFER:**
> *Arrange for
> Dave and Neta
> Jackson to come
> to your school or
> homeschool
> group for a one-
> or two-day
> writing
> seminar.*

Just point your browser to http://www.trailblazerbooks.com

CONTENTS

DAVE AND NETA JACKSON are a full-time husband/wife writing team who have authored and coauthored many books on marriage and family, the church, relationships, and other subjects. Their books for children include the TRAILBLAZER series and *Hero Tales,* volumes I, II, and III. The Jacksons have two married children, Julian and Rachel, and make their home in Evanston, Illinois.

Chapter 1

"Chicken Lottie"

MOLLIE JONES TAPPED HER TOE impatiently behind the counter of Jones's Emporium as a woman in a gray pinstripe tailored dress and flat-brimmed straw hat fingered the bolt of pink chambray cloth. Couldn't Mrs. Meriweather make up her mind?

Mollie sneaked a glance at the shelf below the counter where her father had tossed the new *Ladies Wear Catalog, Fall 1893*, still in its brown paper wrapping. She was dying to open it—but Papa would skin her alive if she ignored a customer and missed a sale. He'd gone to Richmond on a buying trip and wouldn't be back till late. She could close the store soon—

if it wasn't for Mrs. Meriweather.

On the other hand, the woman *did* have a certain handsome older son. . . . It might pay to be nice.

"That's a new material we just got in last week, Mrs. Meriweather," she chirped. "It's very fashionable in Boston this summer." Well, she didn't *really* know if it was fashionable in Boston or not, but maybe Mrs. Meriweather would be impressed enough to buy five or six yards. On the other hand, thirteen-year-old Mollie couldn't quite imagine the starchy president of the Women's Missionary Union of Sugar Grove Baptist Church wearing something as soft and lovely as that pink chambr—

Frantic squawks and high-pitched barking shattered the lazy stillness of the warm August afternoon. "My word, what is *that*?" said Mrs. Meriweather.

"The hens!" Mollie yelled and raced into the storeroom at the back of the Emporium. If that stray dog was bothering Chicken Lottie and Moon Chicken again. . . !

Grabbing a straw broom leaning near the back door, Mollie ran outside toward the chicken yard, hollering, "Tom! Dog in the coop!"

Sure enough, a scrawny brown dog was racing around inside the chicken wire, yapping and nipping at the hysterical hens that were bouncing off the fence and colliding with each other in midair in a kind of frantic dance. Feathers and dust churned inside the chicken yard like soup at a full boil.

"Out! Get out, you fleabag!" yelled Mollie, whacking the broom against the chicken wire. But whacking the fence only made the hens more frantic, and one flew right over the top of the fence and landed behind Mollie. By this time Mollie had jerked open the wire-and-wood gate of the chicken yard and marched in, broom in hand. She hesitated just a moment, then latched the gate behind her. If she chased the dog out the gate, she'd *never* know how it got in.

"Mol-*lie*! Are you coming back soon?" Mrs. Meriweather's shrill plea from the back door of the store was like too much pepper in the soup. "Oh, Tom, do go help your sister."

Mollie heard her younger brother come running across the yard. She waved him back and then advanced on the stray dog with the broom. The mongrel cowered. Then, with a last hungry look at the still-fluttering chickens, the dog stuck its nose under a loose spot along the chicken-wire fence, wiggled under it, and took off running.

"So *that's* where you got in," Mollie murmured, shaking the loose fence. The wire had pulled free from some of the nails holding it to the nearest fence post.

"Hey, Mollie, ain't this Ida Baker's chicken? I think mebbe it's hurt."

Ten-year-old Tom was holding the hen that had flown out of the chicken yard. A smirk creased his freckled face from ear to ear.

"Well, if it is, it's not funny!" Mollie snapped, counting nine hens bunching and complaining in the corner of the yard before letting herself out and latching the gate again.

Tom was still grinning. "Ain't the hen that's funny. *You* are. You're going to scare Papa's customers away."

Mollie glanced down at the once-white apron that she wore in the store to cover her plain gingham dress. Both dress and apron were now rumpled and dirty, and her black button shoes were covered with dust and chicken feathers. Her hair ribbon had come untied, and wild corkscrews of straw-colored hair were hanging in her face.

She tossed her head. "Don't care. Got rid of the dog, didn't I?"

"Mol-*lie!*" called Mrs. Meriweather again. "Are you coming back now?"

"In a minute, Mrs. Meriweather." Mollie bent close to Tom to examine the wide-eyed hen in his arms. "Oh dear. It *is* Moon Chicken. Ida will be upset. . . . Do you think it's badly hurt?"

Tom shrugged. "Dunno. It was flopping like it hurt its leg."

"Mol-*lie!*"

"I'm *coming!*" Frustrated, Mollie resorted to begging. "Tom, be a good brother and take Ida's hen to Mama—she'll know what to do. And don't go running to tell Ida, you hear me? No sense getting her all upset if it's just a little sprain. But I gotta go, or Mrs. Meriweather will complain to Papa when he gets back!"

Mollie ran into the storeroom behind Jones's Emporium as Tom's voice carried after her, "Okay, but you owe me a favor!" She quickly pumped water into the sink to wash her hands and face, and retied her hair ribbon. Ida Baker was Mollie's best friend. The only child of Pastor and Mrs. Baker, Ida lived with her parents in the parsonage of the Sugar Grove Baptist Church, which had no yard and no chicken coop. So Ida kept her "missionary chicken" in the chicken coop behind Jones's Emporium, along with the nine other chickens, one for each member of the Jones family: Mollie, her Mama and Papa, brother Tom, eight-year-old Janice, the twins—Beth and Bonnie—age five, three-year-old Isaiah, and baby Mary. Ten chickens, but only Tom, Mollie, and Ida could sell their eggs. The rest of the eggs were used for cooking and baking.

A few minutes later Mollie had cut and wrapped six yards of the pink chambray for Mrs. Meriweather. "That will be one dollar and ninety cents, please."

Mrs. Meriweather counted out two dollars from her cloth handbag. "You have the makings of a right smart young businesswoman, Mollie Jones ... though you simply mustn't leave a customer standing here cooling her heels while you run off to chase chickens."

Mollie gave her two nickels in change. "I'm truly sorry, Mrs. Meriweather." The customer was *always* right, Papa said. But she couldn't help adding slyly, "But I didn't want that stray dog to get our *missionary chickens*, or we wouldn't have any egg money to put in the Christmas offering for Lottie Moon."

Mollie knew *that* would pacify Mrs. Meriweather. Lottie Moon was the darling of the Women's Missionary Union—their very own missionary to China, born right here in Virginia. An unmarried woman, at that! Not that any of them had ever met her. But everyone had heard of Lottie Moon. Why, Miss Moon wrote articles about China for *The Religious Herald,* and it was because of her that the women in Southern Baptist churches had organized Women's Missionary Unions to support their missionaries. Sugar Grove also had a Sunbeam Band for children, so they could help raise money, too.

"Oh!" Mrs. Meriweather's face actually beamed. "I will tell you a secret.... Well, it's not really a secret, but I only got the letter today and haven't even had a chance to tell Pastor Baker yet." She leaned forward and spoke to Mollie as if passing along a confidence. "Lottie Moon has come home on furlough, you know, and has ever so many invitations to speak. But I wrote and told her our Sugar Grove WMU is one of her most *loyal* supporters. And do you know? She has agreed to speak at our regular meeting Friday next! Isn't that wonderful? We will invite the Sunbeam Band, too, of course! Oh my—I really must go over and talk to Pastor Baker right away."

Mrs. Meriweather bustled out of the store, mumbling, "I do wonder if I can get this dress made by next Friday...."

Mollie stared after the gray tailored dress. Lottie Moon was coming *here*, to Sugar Grove?

With Mrs. Meriweather gone, Mollie locked up the dry goods store, and a few hours later she and Ida were sprawled on Ida's bed in the little attic bedroom of the parsonage—luckily it was Tom's night to do the dishes, and Mama had let Mollie go.

"I never actually thought of Lottie Moon as a real person, did you?" she said, reverently turning the pages of the new *Ladies Wear Catalog* that lay between them. Ida was doodling dress designs on a sketch pad. "I mean, she went to China before we were *born*. She must be really *old* now. Ooo, look at *that* dress, Ida!" Mollie pointed to a royal blue dress with billowing leg-o'-mutton sleeves, a hint of white lace at the edge of the throat, wrists, and hemline, and a wide crimson belt.

Ida's dark brown eyes widened. "Look at that small waist!" Ida's thick chestnut-colored hair was caught up at the sides with a hair ribbon, like Mollie's, with a short crop of bangs on her forehead, and long hair falling down her back.

"She's wearing a corset, you goose!" Mollie said triumphantly. "Mama said I can have one when I'm fourteen."

Ida frowned. "Don't know if I want one. That model looks like she can't breathe."

"Fiddlesticks!" scoffed Mollie. "All the women wear them. And you *have* to wear one if you want to wear some of the newest fashions." She idly turned another page—then suddenly stopped and stared at her friend. "Ida! Do you think . . . ? Oh no. I *must* get Tom to promise not to tell Miss Moon that we named our missionary chickens 'Chicken Lottie' and 'Moon Chicken' after her."

Ida's hand flew to her mouth. "He wouldn't!"

"Oh, he would . . . but he won't. If he does, I'll tell Mama that he spent all his egg money on a pocket-knife instead of putting it in the mission offering last Christmas."

"At least Moon Chicken isn't really hurt. Your

mama said she only sprained her leg flying out of the coop. But, Mollie . . ." Ida looked troubled. "Do you think *we're* doing the right thing, only giving *some* of our egg money to the mission offering?"

Mollie sat up straight. "Ida! Of course it's all right. No one ever said we had to give *all* of it to the mission offering. We've been very faithful about tithing it, after all." Mollie bounced off the narrow bed and snatched up a tin bank that sat on Ida's chest of drawers. "Aren't you excited about all the money we've saved to buy honest-to-goodness catalog dresses just alike? We've almost got enough, don't you think?" She rattled Ida's bank. "But I want to wait until Mama lets me wear my dresses a longer length. She still treats me like a *child* instead of a young lady. . . .

"And that's another thing, Ida Baker. I don't think we should have to go to the Sunbeam Band anymore. All those baby songs we sing . . ." Mollie pitched her voice in falsetto as she sang, " 'Jesus wants me for a sunbeam, to shine for Him each daaay.' " She rolled her green eyes. "We've been singing that song at Sunbeam Band since we were *six*. But we're thirteen now, almost grown!"

Ida giggled. "I don't really mind. At least we get to meet with the ladies when Lottie Moon comes to visit on Friday."

"Uh-huh," Mollie murmured, her eyes catching sight of a pale green dress with a layered skirt and high, puffed sleeves. "Ida, look at *that* one. . . ."

✧ ✧ ✧

Sugar Grove Baptist Church was packed the following Friday night—and the men hadn't even been invited. The room was hot, even with all the windows opened, and the cardboard fans provided in the pews with the hymnbooks were busy. Mollie scorned the second pew where her mother, brothers, and sisters were sitting. Dragging Ida by the hand, she squeezed into a back row with some of the older girls and young ladies.

"Mama doesn't like me to sit in the back rows," Ida whispered nervously. "She says the backsliders sit back here."

"Oh, fiddlesticks," Mollie whispered back. "*We're* not backsliders, and *we're* sitting here." She craned her neck, looking at the row of ladies sitting up on the small platform. The pulpit had been removed, and a row of large potted plants on the edge of the platform created a low wall where ladies could sit without their ankles or petticoats showing. "Wonder where Miss Moon is? Maybe she didn't come, after all."

Mrs. Meriweather, decked out from neck to shoe top in pink chambray and looking a little like a dish of whipped meringue, stood and coughed politely behind a gloved hand. Mollie held her nose and tried not to laugh, but her efforts soon had Ida giggling helplessly.

"The Women's Missionary Union of Sugar Grove Baptist Church is just *thrilled* to have as our speaker this evening none other than our very own Miss Lottie Moon, all the way from . . . from . . . where is it, dear? Yes, from Tengchow, in China. Miss Moon has nobly given up all the comforts of home to take the Gospel to the poor, heathen Chinese. Let's all give her a very big welcome." Mrs. Meriweather beamed and patted her gloved hands daintily together.

All the women and children stood and clapped. Mollie clapped vigorously, giving the giggles a chance to escape.

They all sat down. But still Mollie didn't see Lottie Moon.

Then a short figure stood up from where she'd been hidden behind a bushy philodendron. Mollie's jaw dropped. The famous Miss Lottie Moon was no taller than her eight-year-old sister, Janice—and Janice was only four foot three! Miss Moon's black hair was streaked with silver and piled in a bun on her head, above a simple white shirtwaist with sleeves badly out of fashion, and a plain black skirt. Her figure was round and a little roly-poly, like a . . . like a . . .

"Why, Ida!" Mollie hissed in her friend's ear. "Miss Moon looks just like Chicken Lottie to me!"

Ida's eyes widened. "Oh, Mollie, you really are wicked!" And then the giggles took over the two girls again.

Miss Moon just stood behind the row of greenery until the murmurs and shuffling quieted down. Mollie caught a glimpse of Ida's father, Pastor Baker, standing in the back, so she did her best to stifle the giggles and put a reverent look on her face.

Finally the missionary spoke. "I bring you greetings from the church in Tengchow, your brothers and sisters in Christ."

Mollie was surprised at the low, rich voice. Not at all like the shrill Mrs. Meriweather's.

"Before I begin, I would like to clear up a misconception. The Chinese are *not* heathens." Miss Moon paused. "Unsaved, yes; but *not* uncivilized. We Americans need to be reminded that China was the most civilized nation on earth when our Anglo-Saxon forbearers were still lurking in the forests of northern Europe!"

Mrs. Meriweather's cardboard fan seemed to flutter faster in front of her face as the visiting missionary squared her shoulders and took a deep breath. Though short in stature, Lottie Moon's presence seemed to fill the room. "My dear sisters, isn't it time that we followers of Jesus revise our language and learn to speak respectfully of non-Christian peoples?"

Chapter 2

Sea Worms

THE ROOM FULL OF FANNING WOMEN and whispering children inside Sugar Grove Baptist Church was startled into stillness . . . except for a pesky fly that buzzed around the lady's hat in front of Mollie and Ida. Mollie was torn between a peevish delight that Mrs. Meriweather had virtually been scolded in public, and thinking maybe she hadn't heard right. Of *course* the Chinese were heathen! On that point she decided she agreed with Mrs. Meriweather. Why, in China they worshiped that fat Buddha idol and ate their food with sticks and who knew what other heathen things.

Lottie Moon continued quietly. "When I first went to China, I considered the Chinese an

21

inferior race. Everything was so strange! Their food, their houses, their customs, their language, their clothes . . . and I liked *my* food and *my* clothes and *my* customs much better!"

Hats nodded, and murmurs of relief rippled through the pews. Mollie relaxed. She knew what her mother and Mrs. Meriweather and the other ladies were thinking. Now Miss Moon was making sense. Of *course* Western civilization was superior to pagan cultures like China. And wasn't Lottie Moon born and bred right here in Virginia? *Southern* culture—now, *that* was the cream in the coffee. Mama always said, "You can take a Virginia girl out of the South, but you can't take the South out of a Virginia girl!"

Well, Mollie had her own opinions on *that*. Someday she wanted to travel and see the world. But it wouldn't be to go see some old backward country like China. She wanted to see Paris and London and—

". . . but when I finally put on Chinese clothes and slept in a Chinese house and ate Chinese food," Miss Moon was saying, "the people stopped calling me a 'foreign devil' and started listening when I told them Jesus died to save them, too."

Whispers buzzed up and down the pews. "Foreign devil?" "How insulting!"

At the front of the church, Lottie Moon smiled like she knew a good joke. "And I have to tell you this—boxy Chinese trousers and coats are a lot more comfortable than this insufferable corset I've had to wear since I've been back home!"

No one laughed. Even Mollie was shocked. She had *never* heard the word "corset" mentioned in church before. Whatever would Ida's father think?

The evening flew by quickly. No one knew what Miss Moon was going to say next! She told stories about the sufferings of little girls whose feet were bound in tight rags and not allowed to grow because tiny feet were considered beautiful in China. Mollie's and Ida's mouths gaped as they tried to imagine standing up on itty-bitty feet that were only three inches long.

Miss Moon's dark eyes danced as she described "country work"—going village to village to tell the simple farming families about Jesus. "The people are so hungry to hear God loves them and so grateful that we have come to tell them this good news!"

She smiled. "But I do confess. The hardest thing about country work was learning to eat what was set before me. I'm afraid I drew the line at sea worms— even though they are considered a great delicacy in China."

Sea worms! Mollie poked Ida and pretended to gag.

"As you've probably noticed," Miss Moon said wryly, "I am no longer a young woman. I am very tired when I get back to Tengchow after visiting these villages. But in twenty years we have visited only a fraction of the villages in Shangtung Province. There are still millions of Chinese who have never heard the name of Jesus."

Behind her glasses, her dark eyes flashed, and

Mollie thought Miss Moon would almost be pretty, if she paid just a little more attention to her clothes.

"Because of Chinese custom," Miss Moon said soberly, "it is not proper for a man—especially a foreign man!—to teach the women. And most of the female missionaries are married, with their own

24

responsibilities for family and children. But this is a fact: Only women can reach Chinese women for Christ! I beg you, my sisters, pray that God will send more workers into the harvest!"

Heads nodded all around the room. But the missionary looked around with a sad smile. "I see several young women here, and older girls. When I was your age, I know what I was dreaming about—finding a dashing young beau, getting married, and having at least six children."

Mollie poked Ida in the ribs. "A dashing beau, yes," she whispered, "but *you* can have the six children!" Ida was always telling Mollie how lucky she was to have so many brothers and sisters. But as far as Mollie was concerned, she'd take being an only child any day!

"But, dear young people," said Miss Moon, "maybe *you* are the very person Jesus is calling to be His hands and feet in China! Have you ever thought of your singleness as a gift God can use on the mission field?"

Again the room was very quiet. Mollie ducked her head and rolled her eyes. Being a missionary was all right for Miss Moon, who probably would have been an old maid anyway, but why would any young woman in her right mind *choose* not to get married and go work her fingers to the bone in some forgotten corner of the world? Not Mollie, that was for sure!

"We here in America take our blessings for granted," the low, rich voice continued. "I am jealous—yes, jealous!—that here in Virginia, there are hundreds of churches just like Sugar Grove Baptist Church, each with its own pastor. But in China, there is only a handful of pastors to preach the Word to millions of lost men and women. Oh, dear sisters, dear young people, I beg you . . . whether or not God is calling *you* to the mission field, *give* from your abundant resources to send more missionaries to tell a lost world about Jesus. We simply cannot keep the Good News for ourselves."

Mollie felt a movement at her side and realized Ida was slipping out of the pew. *Where are you going?* she mouthed silently to her friend.

Ida just held up her hand and mouthed, *I'll be right back.*

Mollie looked toward the front and realized Miss Moon had sat down, disappearing behind the wall of potted plants. Mrs. Meriweather stood up, flushed and looking a little relieved that she was once again in control.

But where did Ida go? Mollie twisted in her seat and looked toward the back. Ida was talking with her father; then she slipped out the side door that led toward the church parsonage. Why was Ida going home?

". . . saving nickels and dimes for the Christmas Offering for Missions," Mrs. Meriweather was saying, a ruffled pink contrast to Lottie Moon's simple presence. "But Christmas is several months away. Let's show Miss Moon that Sugar Grove Baptist WMU is one hundred percent committed to sending more missionaries to China by taking a special offer-

26

ing tonight. This includes you children in the Sunshine Band, too. Please give generously. Boys?"

Mrs. Meriweather nodded at Mollie's brother Tom and another boy to come to the front and get the offering baskets. Miss Lilly Locke went to the little pump organ and played "In Christ There Is No East or West" while the baskets went around. Mollie squirmed. She had ten cents in the little cloth purse that hung from her wrist—her share of the eggs she and Ida had sold that week. One penny—ten percent—was supposed to go in her missions box, but nine cents was going into her savings that she kept in her bottom drawer. If she gave the penny to missions now—no, she couldn't do that because all she had was two nickles. She'd have to give a nickel if she gave anything at all. But if she did that, she could pay herself back four cents from her missions box. . . .

While Mollie was pondering what to give to the special offering, Ida squeezed back into the pew and plopped into her place beside Mollie. "Where did you go?" Mollie demanded in a whisper. "They're taking a special offering for missions."

"I know," Ida whispered back. "That's why I went home." She held up her tin bank.

Mollie stared at the tin bank, then looked sharply at Ida. Whatever was Ida thinking? That was her dress money! The money they'd been saving for two years to buy identical dresses from the *Ladies Wear Catalog*!

Just then Tom showed up at the end of their pew with the offering basket, looking warm and uncomfortable in his stand-up collar and tie and short dress pants. He smirked at his sister as he started the basket down her row.

But Mollie was too distracted to glare back. She felt like a twig in a lazy creek that was suddenly tumbling over a waterfall. Things were happening too fast! She saw Ida open her bank and empty its contents into the wicker offering basket. Mollie felt trapped. How could she give "just" her nickel now? A minute ago, a nickel had seemed extra generous— four cents *more* than a tithe of what she had in her purse. But now Ida had gone and dumped ten *dollars* into the offering basket!

Furious, Mollie dug into her cloth purse and came up with the two nickels that had been snuggling in the bottom with her hanky and a pair of gloves that she'd put in there to make it look bulky. She threw the coins in the basket as it went past, then stared straight ahead and refused to look at Ida.

Every time Mollie thought of what Ida had done, she got mad all over again. She could hardly think of anything else. All those months selling eggs and saving their money, all their plans to buy matching dresses . . . and *poof!* Ida gave her savings away, just like that! And they hadn't even talked about it! She just did it—what kind of friend was that?

"Please don't be upset," Ida had said after the meeting. "You can still buy yourself a dress. I . . . I just decided I would rather use my savings to help a missionary go to China than get a new dress."

But Mollie *was* upset. Of course she could still buy a new dress with her egg money savings. That wasn't the point! They had planned to buy *matching* dresses—that was the fun of it! Weren't they best friends? Didn't everyone call them "the Sugar Grove Twins"? It would have been so much fun to have matching outfits from the *Ladies Wear Catalog* . . . and now Ida had ruined it all.

As Mollie lay on her bed that night in the small room over the store that she shared with Janice and the twins, staring at the chintz curtains moving gently at the open window, she realized what was *really* bothering her. Ida had humiliated her, that's what! By putting so much money into the special offering, she made Mollie look selfish only putting in ten cents. But it wasn't fair! That was all she had in her purse right then. And even though Ida didn't say so, Mollie felt like Ida was looking down her nose at her because she didn't put in *her* dress money, too. And the ladies who'd been sitting on either side of them at the meeting were probably talking about them right now: "What a wonderful girl Pastor Baker's daughter is! So much more generous than that stingy Mollie Jones."

Whomp! Mollie punched her pillow—hard—then pulled the blanket over her head and silently cried herself to sleep.

The next day was Saturday, and Mama and Papa kept her busy all day. Mollie was just as glad, because that gave her a good excuse for staying away from the Bakers' house. She didn't want to see Ida. Not today, not tomorrow—maybe not ever!

All morning she worked in the store with her father, stocking the shelves with the goods he'd brought back from Richmond earlier that week. Her anger simmered just below the surface, and she stacked boxes of wooden pencils, cards of ribbon and fancy braid, and jars of pickled herring with equal recklessness. Papa, trim and businesslike with his neatly clipped reddish gray hair, striped shirt, and string tie, was busy with customers and didn't seem to notice. But then, Haley Jones often seemed too busy to notice.

In the afternoon, Mollie Jones had to baby-sit baby Mary, Isaiah, and the twins while Mama put up a "Back to School" display in the front window of the Emporium. Normally, Mollie would have packed her youngest siblings in their wobbly child's wagon— badly in a need of a coat of paint—and pulled them over to the Bakers' house. Ida loved playing with the babies, and she made baby-sitting much easier. But today Mollie just sat and watched the little ones splash in Mama's washtub out in the backyard.

It was Ida's turn to come over and collect eggs tomorrow morning before church. Well, Mollie would just be "busy" when Ida came to the back door.

When Mollie got to church the next morning, wearing her best summer-weight shirtwaist, starched crisp and ironed just that morning, with her favorite blue-flowered skirt, she pretended to not notice Ida, who was sitting with her mother in the first row on the right. The Jones family usually sat on the left in the second row. Mollie glanced casually in Ida's direction and was a little startled to see that Ida's eyes looked red, like she'd been crying.

Guilt tickled the edges of Mollie's anger. Was Ida crying because Mollie was mad at her?

All during the morning service, the resentment Mollie had been feeling toward Ida leaked out of her spirit like milky whey dripping from the cloth bag when her mother made cheese. It had been taking a lot of energy to stay mad at Ida. Maybe . . . maybe this afternoon she'd take Beth and Bonnie for a walk and "just happen" to go by the parsonage, and Ida would see them and come running out and beg Mollie to forgive her for being so thoughtless, and she would say nobly, "Of course I forgive you, Ida!" and they would fall into each other's arms and—

"Before I close, I have something important I need to say to the congregation," Pastor Baker was saying.

Mollie's head jerked up. Was the morning service over already? She focused on Pastor Baker, standing behind the white-painted pulpit, and tried to look as though she had been paying attention all along. He was a pleasant-looking man with dark hair like Ida, a full moustache, and serious eyes. This morning Ida's father looked even more serious. Had someone died?

"As most of you know, the Women's Missionary Union and the Sunbeam Band had the privilege of

31

hearing the remarkable Miss Lottie Moon two days ago. As pastor, they let me eavesdrop—though I had to keep quiet and stand in the back." He grinned, and laughter rippled through the little congregation. "But Friday night Miss Moon opened my eyes to the desperate need for missionary pastors in the vast land of China. Her challenge cut to my heart, and all weekend I have been wrestling with God's call on my life."

Mollie shot another glance at Ida across the aisle. What was Pastor Baker talking about? But Ida was staring at her lap.

"This will seem very sudden to you all—but time is short. I spoke to Miss Moon and she is confident I will qualify as a missionary candidate." Pastor Baker paused and gripped the sides of the white pulpit. "If the mission board accepts me, at the end of September I will be resigning as pastor of Sugar Grove Baptist Church. In November, I hope to sail with Miss Moon to China, along with my wife, Nellie, and our daughter, Ida."

A startled gasp swept up and down the rows of pews. But Mollie felt as though someone had punched her in the stomach and knocked all the breath out of her.

Ida Baker, her very own best friend in the whole world since they were *babies*, was going to move away from Sugar Grove? Not just leave Sugar Grove, but leave Nelson County? Leave Virginia? Leave America?—and go clear to the other side of the world to that . . . that godless, heathen, ugly country where they eat *sea worms*?

Chapter 3

The Pen Pal Pledge

MOLLIE'S INSIDES FELT TWISTED and drained from crying—like the sheets and towels on washing day after Mama had wrung out the last possible drop of rinse water before hanging them on the clothesline.

At first it had seemed too unbelievable to be true. But at the end of September, Pastor Thomas Baker preached his last sermon, and then traveled by train to Richmond to meet with the Southern Baptist Mission Board and get travel documents and tickets for the Baker family. The oak, maple, and birch trees on the hillsides turned brilliant reds, yellows, and oranges as Sugar Grove Baptist limped through

October with first this preacher and then that one "filling the pulpit."

Their quarrel quickly forgotten—what did matching dresses matter if Ida wasn't even going to be there to wear it?—the two friends spent every possible moment together. School had started, but Mollie and Ida spent half the time slipping notes between their desks, and even the teacher pretended not to notice.

Ida poured out her fears to Mollie in the dark as the two girls "slept over" as often as their parents would let them. "I don't want to go to China," Ida often cried. "I . . . I just want to be a normal girl and stay in Sugar Grove and . . . and get married someday and have a big family like yours. Oh, Mollie, it's going to be so lonely. At least if *you* were going to China, you'd have Tom and Janice and the babies to play with."

For once, Mollie didn't know what to say. Her own emotions were all in a jumble. Sometimes she thought she wouldn't be able to bear it when Ida left. She couldn't imagine life in Sugar Grove without her best friend. Ida was always . . . *there*. Didn't Ida stick up for her when the teacher thought *she* was the one who put a frog in her desk? Who else would have gone along with Mollie's idea to dress up as "Mother Goose" and "Old Mother Hubbard" with all the Jones children in tow—well, except Tom, who wouldn't cooperate—for Sugar Grove's Fourth of July parade? Who else could she trust not to tell a *soul* about her secret crush on Mrs. Meriweather's oldest son, George?

At other times Mollie felt jealous. Why was God sending Ida, of all people, halfway around the world? Ida didn't have an adventurous bone in her body! Mollie was the one with grand ideas, the one who wanted to travel the world someday—well, maybe not to dreary old China, but still. *She* should be the one setting out on an adventure to the unknown. And she would manage very well without all her brothers and sisters, thank you.

But now it was November, and in two days the Bakers were leaving by train for San Francisco, where they would meet Lottie Moon and board the *Empress of China*. Furniture had been sold or stored; boxes were packed. Ida's parents were upstairs in the Jones's apartment above the Emporium, drinking tea with Mollie's parents and checking off last-minute lists.

Mollie and Ida sat on the back steps watching the twilight swallow up the houses of Sugar Grove. Indian summer was lingering, but nightfall had sucked the warmth out of the air and left a bright, chilly moon sparkling in the sky. The girls huddled together under one of Mrs. Jones's quilts, wrapped in sadness.

"I begged Daddy to let me stay with you," sniffed Ida. "But he wouldn't hear of it."

Mollie's heart leaped. "Oh! I *know* Mama and Papa wouldn't mind. Why, they'd hardly notice one more! We'd be just like sisters!"

Ida didn't answer. They both knew it wasn't going to happen.

The silence lengthened. An idea started spinning in Mollie's head. Just like sisters . . . Why not? She wiggled out of the quilt and jumped up. "Let's do it!"

"Do what?" The expression on Ida's face was the familiar mixture of wariness and willingness she usually greeted Mollie's ideas with.

"Become soul sisters! Wait . . . I'll show you."

Mollie ran up the outside stairs to their apartment over the store. She opened the back door quietly, lifted the storeroom key off its little hook, and crept back down the stairs to where Ida was waiting wrapped in the quilt. "Come on," she whispered.

Unlocking the back door of the store, Mollie felt around until she found the kerosene lantern and the box of matches on the shelf. Striking a match, she lifted the glass chimney and held it to the wick. The shadows in the storeroom backed into the corners.

Mollie rummaged in a drawer, then said, "Aha. Here they are." She held up a long pair of scissors used for cutting cloth, silver and shiny in the lamplight. She looked soberly into Ida's questioning eyes. "If you wear a lock of someone's hair next to your heart, that person becomes part of you in a special way. It's like a promise that holds you together, stronger than your own family."

With the lamplight flickering in her green eyes, Mollie pulled a lock of hair from underneath her mop of curls. With a snip, the straw-colored ringlet fell into her hand. "This is for you, Ida—to wear next to your heart. Now . . . cut one for me." She handed the scissors to Ida.

Snip. A moment later Ida handed a lock of her own dark chestnut hair to Mollie. "Soul sisters," she whispered . . . then suddenly burst into tears. "Oh, Mollie, I will write to you every week! Promise me you'll write back? I will die if I don't hear from you!"

Mollie's frowsy curls bobbed up and down. "I promise. Pen pals *forever*."

Ida Baker gripped her pencil as the passenger car of the Union Pacific Railroad swayed rhythmically. It was so hard to write on a train! But she had promised Mollie, and it had been three whole days since they'd left Sugar Grove.

The scenery outside the smoky train window was flat and barren. Ida had only a vague idea of where they were—Kansas or Nebraska or someplace like that. The flat land went on for mile after dreary mile—nothing at all like the beautiful rolling hills of Virginia. Sometimes she couldn't see even a single tree! Inside the coach car, Ida's mother was dozing in the padded seat next to her, her gloved hands resting on the wicker picnic basket that held the remains of their travel food—hard-boiled eggs, smoked turkey, Boston brown bread, sweet yellow apples, and dried peaches. Ida's father was also dozing in the seat across the aisle, looking rather small beside the enormous man squeezed into the seat next to him.

For a moment Ida fingered the locket she was wearing with the lock of Mollie's hair . . . then

she steadied the sheet of writing paper on the book in her lap, licked the tip of her pencil, and began.

Dearest Mollie,

Please pardon this wretched pencil, but an inkpot and pen is out of the question on this rocking horse called a train! For a desk I am using the beautiful book your parents gave me as a good-bye present. Anna Sewell is now my favorite author! But the story of Black Beauty is so sad, I want to weep. How can men treat God's creatures so cruelly?

My heart beats with Black Beauty—even if he is a horse!—because he was taken away against his will from the home he loved, and he was lonely and afraid. Oh, Mollie, my heart grows heavier each day as every click of the big iron wheels underneath me take me farther and farther away from Sugar Grove.

There is not much to write about yet. We traveled first to Richmond, then to Washington, D.C.—oh, Mollie, I thought of you! I saw many fashionable women in the Washington train station—and such hats! Purple and gold turbans, very exotic—nothing like the straw sailor hats so common in Sugar Grove. However, the train station is all I saw of the capital. We didn't dare leave our luggage and had to stay beside it until it was time to board the Baltimore and Ohio going west. We changed trains again in St. Louis—I think we stay on the Union Pacific now clear to San Francisco.

Tell your mother that the Boston brown bread is still very moist and good. But I am a little tired of the same food from our basket. Daddy says tonight we shall eat in the dining car—I am very excited. I peeked into the dining car—it has white tablecloths and padded chairs and a rose on every table! The people eating there looked very sophisticated. That shall be me tonight!

I can't think of anything else to write. Sorry about the smudges. I have no eraser. But I will add to this later.

Pacific Ocean
November 23, 1893

Oh, Mollie! Never in my wildest dreams did I imagine a ship as big as the Empress of China! We have been on board two days now, and I still haven't explored the whole ship. We met Miss Moon in San Francisco—good thing! She speaks Chinese very well and can tell us what the crew is saying. What strange, twangy sounds they make! The captain and chief steward speak English, though, and everyone is very polite. The Empress carries a lot of cargo, so there are not many passengers. But we are treated like royalty! (I wonder if they know we're just country folks? I hope they don't find out!)

I hate feeling ignorant—but that's how I feel when I don't know what people are saying and can't read signs. Yesterday I went exploring, and opened a door on one of the lower decks. A big, bald man (except for a long pigtail down his back) yelled something at me and pushed me right out again. He frightened me. Later Miss Moon told me the sign on the door said Danger—Keep Out. It led to the big coal furnaces that power the steam engines. I felt so stupid.

Daddy says I must learn to read and write Chinese. But it seems impossible! At least when we studied French in school, the letters were the same and I could sound out the words.

Back again! As you see, I can use pen and ink now, because most of the time sailing is very smooth. But sometimes the ocean swells send Miss Moon to her cabin looking very green. I like Miss Moon—she is quite fun! Last night at supper (we eat at the captain's table) she told us stories about taking her niece Maime to the Chicago World's Fair last month. They rode a big wheel (called a Ferris wheel, I think) that was taller than any building in Sugar Grove, even the grain elevator! The wheel didn't go anywhere, just around and around, but Miss Moon said she and Maime could see the whole city of Chicago from the top. At night the whole fair was lit with electric lights—can you imagine?

The weather is getting very hot. The captain says we are going to stop at the Sandwich Islands in a day or two. I once saw pictures in a book about the Islands— lots of palm trees and pearl white beaches and girls with orchids in their long black hair. I can hardly believe I will see them for myself. But it would be so much more fun if you were here.

Miss Moon seems very excited to be going back to China. Daddy hangs on every word she says. I don't know what Mama thinks. She is trying to be brave and interested. But I think she is scared, like me.

Tengchow, Shantung Province, China
December 25, 1893

Oh, Mollie, I am so lonely I think I will die. Today is Christmas Day—but the Chinese do not celebrate Christmas! I don't care what Miss Moon says. That seems heathen to me!

But at least Miss Moon invited the other missionaries here in Tengchow to come to her house for a "Christmas dinner." (Her home is called Little Cross Roads, and it is SO enchanting! It sits in the middle of a walled garden and has a red-tile roof, very Chinese.) Some of the Chinese Christians came, too, wearing beautiful embroidered silk robes. After dinner we sang Christmas carols, and Miss Moon read the Christmas story in both English and Chinese.

Still, it was nothing like Christmas back in Virginia! Remember last Christmas Eve when George Meriweather let us girls ride along in his dad's sleigh when he went to cut down the Christmas tree for the church? What a glorious ride! The only sound was the heavy breathing of the horses and the sleigh bells tinkling with each crunch of their hooves. I thought you were going to swoon with happiness! (Don't worry—I never told anyone about your secret crush on George, even though you know he's too old for you—he's at least sixteen.)

We had no stockings to hang last night—not even a fireplace to hang them on! Last Christmas I had no idea that this year I would be halfway around the world, in a country where Christmas Day is just like any other ordinary day.

But I'm getting too far ahead of myself. So much has happened in the last few weeks! We arrived in Shanghai December 14 and were treated very kindly by the American missionaries there (even though they are Presbyterian, not Baptist). We took another ship—not so large—to Chefoo and then traveled overland the last forty miles to Tengchow. You will never believe how we traveled! By shentze—a contraption that looks like a basket tipped over on its side, with the opening facing forward, slung on two long poles that are carried by two mules, one in front and one in back. Inside are big, thick blankets and rugs, but riding inside was worse than the worst day at sea, tossing back and forth! I was sure I would be black-and-blue from head to toe! And it was so cold—on the way we ran into a snowstorm, almost a blizzard. But the mule drivers kept going. I don't know how they could see the road. But we got to Tengchow safely, and I was so glad to get to Little Cross Roads. Somehow it felt safe to be in Lottie Moon's very own house.

But the beds are so strange! The big brick oven in the kitchen heats the whole house by a large pipe that carries warm air to the other rooms. The bed in each room is just a flat, brick shelf called a kang, with a thick blanket spread on top, heated underneath by the warm air from the kitchen stove. Miss Moon says that in most Chinese homes, the whole family sleeps on one kang. But Miss Moon has a spare room—though it feels funny to be sleeping in the same room as my parents. I haven't done that since I was a little girl!

The first morning I got up early and thought the Chinese cook was making tea—but it was Miss Moon herself, dressed in embroidered cloth slippers and a blue Chinese robe that almost covered her black skirt! She laughed at my face—my mouth must have been hanging open like a goldfish. With her black hair pulled back into a knot, she looks very Chinese.

It unsettles my mother. I overheard her tell Daddy that she thinks Miss Moon is going too far. "A Chris-

tian woman shouldn't go around dressed like a pagan!"
He reminded her that the Christian Chinese women
dress like that, too. She got all flustered and said she
intended to keep her dignity as a civilized American
woman, even if she is in a foreign country.
I don't know . . . what do you think, Mollie?

"Are you writing a book, Ida?" teased a low, pleasant voice.

Ida looked up. Lottie Moon had come into the spare room, where Ida had hidden away to finish her letter. She blushed and shook her head. "Miss Moon, how long will it take a letter to get back to Virginia?"

"Ah, another letter writer! I think China had to hire more mail workers to handle all the letters I write back home! But my letters don't have all those nice little drawings. Hmm, you're quite good, you know." Miss Moon chuckled. "Let's see, if we take your letter to the post tomorrow . . . hmm, your friend might get it by the end of January. We'll go tomorrow morning, all right?"

Ida nodded gratefully. Picking up her pen and dipping it into the inkpot once more, Ida carefully signed her name and blotted it dry. She held the letter for a long moment, blinking hard, trying to imagine Mollie's laughing, freckled face.

True to her word, the next day Miss Moon walked Ida through the narrow cobblestone streets of Tengchow to the little mail office. Ida clung to Lottie Moon like a shadow, threading their way through a seemingly endless stream of pompous men and decorated women riding in rickshaws, peddlers pushing carts and calling out their wares, and women carrying baskets or waterpots from a yoke across their shoulders. Little children, dressed just like their elders in padded coats and trousers, stared at Ida; some pointed and yelled words she could not understand.

Ida had never felt so alone in her entire thirteen years.

Chapter 4

China Moon

MOLLIE WOKE WITH A START as two small bodies jumped on the bed she shared with Janice. "Wake up! Wake up, Mollie!" squealed Bonnie, diving under the warm covers and wiggling between her older sisters.

"It's Christmas!" Beth, the other twin, crowed. "Let's go see the tree!"

"Shh, shh," shushed Mollie, pulling Beth under the covers, too. "We can't go see the tree till Mama and Papa get up."

"But we heard baby Mary cry. Go see! Go see!"

The twins would not be put off. Finally Mollie crawled out of the warm bed, pulled a flannel wrap-

per over her nightgown, and tiptoed down the narrow hall to the boxy sitting room at the front of the
house. Opening the door a crack, she peeked in.
Mama was nursing baby Mary in the rocking chair
that had been re-covered time and time again, and
Papa was carefully lighting the tiny candles on the
freshly cut fir tree that stood in the corner.

Mollie caught Mama's eye, who smiled and nodded, and she was just about to go back and get her
sisters when three pairs of bare feet thundered down
the dark, narrow hall, pushed past Mollie, and burst
into the cozy room. Not far behind them, Tom appeared in his nightshirt, carrying a wide-eyed Isaiah.

The next half hour was filled with squeals of
delight as the seven Jones children dumped trea-
sures out of the much-mended stockings they'd hung
on the old fireplace mantel behind the woodburning
stove. Mollie sifted through her assortment of pep-
permints, walnuts to crack, a new hair ribbon, two
yards of lace to use any way she wanted, three colored drawing pencils, a brand-new twenty-five-cent
piece—enough to buy some linen cuffs she'd seen in
the *Sears, Roebuck Catalogue!*—and last, but not least,
a fragrant bar of Pears Soap. Mollie closed her eyes and
sniffed. That would have been a perfect gift for Ida!

Suddenly she felt sad. Her first-ever Christmas
without Ida.

Mama insisted that they eat breakfast before
opening the brown-paper packages tied with colorful
ends of ribbon and lace under the tree. To the
children's surprise, Mama said they could eat in the

front room with the pungent green tree, cheerfully decorated with paper chains and strings of cranberries. Papa, unusually relaxed on the holiday, helped serve Mama's homemade springle with nutmeats, raisins, and sugar icing, and cups of hot cocoa to go around.

The seven lumpy packages under the tree produced a silver teething ring for baby Mary, a top for Isaiah, rag dolls for the twins, a book for Janice, and a pair of secondhand ice skates for Tom—polished and sharpened and waxed until they looked like new. Papa gave Mama a locket, and she gave him a pair of new suspenders.

Mollie half smiled at her younger brothers and sisters as they opened their gifts, but her mind was elsewhere. For as many Christmases as she could remember, the Bakers had always appeared at their door with a basket of jam, cheese, crackers, and sausage. She and Ida would "Ooo" and "Ahh" over each other's gifts; then they'd play checkers or jacks or paper dolls with the younger ones and—

"Where's Mollie's present?" piped up little Beth.

"Ah!" beamed Papa, snapping his new suspenders. He reached into the branches of the tree, pulled out a square package about the size of a cigar box tied with a mock-velvet ribbon, and handed it to Mollie. "For our young lady."

Mollie gently pulled the ribbon. Young lady? Could it be—? No, the box was too small to be the corset Mama promised her when she turned fourteen. Too big to be a pair of silk stockings. What could it be?

Taking off the brown paper, Mollie lifted the lid of the embossed cardboard box. Inside lay a stack of creamy parchment paper, and at one end snuggled a small bottle of elegant green ink and a long green ink pen. Mollie's eyes widened and her fingers traced some raised printing at the top of the paper. In elegant script it read

Miss Mollie Lucinda Jones
19 Front Street
Sugar Grove, Virginia

"Thought you'd want to do some letter writing now that Ida's gone," her father said, trying to sound matter-of-fact but obviously pleased with his surprise.

"Oh yes, Papa, thank you!" cried Molly, throwing her arms around him. Haley Jones looked a little flustered. He was normally a reserved man.

With a pleading glance at her mother, Mollie slipped out of the noisy sitting room and hurried back into the small bedroom she shared with her sisters. It was colder there, but at least she could be alone for a half hour.

Still in her nightgown and wrapper, Mollie sat cross-legged on the floor and put her new pen and bottle of ink on the little wooden stool the twins used to reach the washbasin. She took out a page of the creamy parchment paper with her name printed at the top and bent over the stool. "Dear Ida . . ." she began.

✧ ✧ ✧

Weeks later, halfway across the world, Ida picked up the letter she had been writing to Mollie and re-read what she had written so far. So much had happened since Christmas! There was so much to tell. . . .

On the road, Shantung Province, China
January 17, 1894

Dearest Mollie,

Miss Moon says you can't have gotten my letter yet, so even if you wrote me, you wouldn't know where to send a letter to me. I tell myself this over and over, but sometimes I'm afraid you have already forgotten me. Oh, Mollie, I never realized how hard it is for a missionary to leave everything familiar and go to a foreign country where EVERYTHING is so strange. I feel like I died and woke up in another world.

And now another change! I thought Daddy was going to work with Miss Moon or some of the other missionaries in Tengchow. Oh, Mollie, I'd love to stay at Little Cross Roads—it felt safe, a place of refuge while we gradually got used to our new life. But Miss Moon says Daddy and Mama are urgently needed in Sha-Ling, a large village about 120 miles from Tengchow. Three men and two women have been baptized there, and at least twenty families meet together in someone's home, but there is no pastor.

But what will we do in Sha-Ling if no one speaks English? We have only just started learning Chinese—a few words here and there. How will we buy food or ask directions? Miss Moon says we can find a teacher in Sha-Ling, "and besides, the best way to learn Chinese is to sink or swim." Huh! She presumes we will "swim." What if we "sink"?

But we are on our way, traveling by two shentzes again. With three pack mules for all our luggage, we make a caravan. (An ordinary horse and carriage in Sugar Grove would seem like a royal coach here in China!) At least I do not feel as seasick this time.

We spent the first night with the Pruitt family in Hwanghsien—they are Americans, too, and welcomed us like long-lost relatives! Mama and Mrs. Pruitt got along famously. (Anna Pruitt is "C. W.'s" second wife and working hard to set up a boarding school for girls.) The Pruitts have two children—a little boy named Ashley, about two, I think, and a little girl named— guess what?—Ida! Just like me. She is only five years old and reminds me so much of the twins. I immediately adopted her as my "little sister" here in China, and I hated so much to leave her the next morning. But I'm sure we will see the Pruitts again.

After we were on the road again, Mama told me that the Pruitts lost a baby a few years ago—and that C. W.'s first wife died only a year after they got married here in China. The farther we travel from Tengchow, the more worried Mama looks. Where would we find a doctor if we get sick? I thought little Ashley Pruitt seemed rather sickly, too. His cheeks had no color, and he didn't run around like Isaiah does. (I can just see Isaiah chasing Chicken Lottie and Moon Chicken, trying to "pet de chickies"!)

The last two nights—oh, Mollie, you can't imagine the dirty, smelly inns we've had to sleep in! All the men sleep in one room on a big, common kang, and Mama and I have to sleep with the women in another. Last night

we shared a kang with an old woman with beady eyes and two young girls only a couple years older than I am. Mollie, you cannot imagine how tiny their feet were, like baby feet, and they walked with teensy steps and kept their eyes on the ground—but I caught them looking at me. Mama thought they were the old woman's daughters, but our mule driver told Daddy that the old woman was First Wife, and the girls were Second Wife and Third Wife! Mama was too shocked for words!

Tonight is our last night in an inn along the way. I am

tired of poached eggs and mein (boiled noodles). Oh, how I'd love some of your mama's biscuits and jam!

Ida sighed. That was while they were still traveling to Shal-Ling. Should she finish the letter? She *still* hadn't heard from Mollie. Maybe Mollie really had forgotten about her.

But inside she knew that couldn't be true. She dipped her pen and added on to the letter she'd started almost two weeks ago.

Sha-Ling, January 28, 1894

Today is Sunday. We have been in Sha-Ling nearly a week. The mission is renting a house for us. It is not as pretty or cozy as Little Cross Roads, but Mama says that when we get our things unpacked and plant some flowers in the garden this spring, that will brighten it up. Like many Chinese houses, it has one main room with a big brick oven for cooking and heating the entire house, and two smaller rooms with sleeping kangs. The front of the house has a small walled garden, but the side of the house is right along one of the main streets of cobblestones. The windows have glass panes that open inward, like French doors (but not fancy at all), and wooden shutters that close from the outside to keep out the cold (and the stares of nosy neighbors).

We can hardly walk anywhere without a crowd of children begging coins from us or wanting to touch my hair or my clothes. I think they're just curious—but sometimes a man or woman will yell at us, and their faces look angry. Then I feel frightened. I wonder if they are calling us "foreign devils," like Miss Moon said.

But Dan Ho-Bang and Mr. Yuan and the other Christians— they are so happy we have come. It makes me feel selfish to complain. Every day someone brings us a basket of rice cakes, apples or dried fruit, or a pot of chicken soup. Mr. Dan said the women washed our house from top to bottom, scrubbing every inch, and spread sweet-smelling straw on all the floors. (Yes! He speaks a little English! At least one of my prayers is answered!) Mr. Dan also arranged for a tutor to come to the house every day to teach us Chinese. His name is Mr. Chiang. Today he gave me a brush and some ink and taught me how to write my name in Chinese. He said, "You are artist—make beautiful letters." I couldn't believe it! For one brief moment I thought—maybe—I would not always feel like a stupid foreigner here in China.

"Ida?" Her father parted the curtain that hung in the doorway of the little room—hardly more than a large pantry—that served as Ida's bedroom. "Did you see the moon? It's the first clear night we've had in a while." Thomas Baker went to the tall, narrow window and pulled the two panels open. "Come and see."

Ida laid down her paper and pen and scooted off the warm shelf covered with a thick quilt that served as her bed, being careful not to knock over the oil lamp that lit the tiny room. A quarter moon was rising over the low, tiled roofs of Sha-Ling. She shivered in the damp, chill air that rushed into the room.

"Today the moon begins its last quarter. Mr. Dan said that the next time the moon is 'new'—when we can't see it at all—it will be time to celebrate the

Chinese New Year."

Ida was only half listening. The moon . . . She had often seen moons just like this one in Sugar Grove. Her heart beat a little faster.

"Daddy, if the sky is clear in Virginia, could Mollie see this same moon tonight?"

Pastor Baker's full, dark moustache curved in a smile. "Well, 'tonight' is still daytime in Virginia, so she couldn't see it right this minute. But, yes, in about twelve hours she'll be able to see this same moon. Now—" Ida's father closed the windows and twisted the latch—"time for bed, young lady. I'm going outside to close up the wooden shutters."

Ida stood looking at the quarter moon for another minute; then crawling back up on the kang, she picked up her pen and dipped it in her inkpot.

Tonight I looked at the moon as if seeing it for the first time since I've been in China. And I realized it is the only thing that is not different about this strange country. It looks familiar and dear, the very same moon we were looking at that night we became soul sisters. For the first time since we arrived in China a month ago, I felt close to you again. Oh, Mollie, the moon is ours! Whenever you look at the moon, tell yourself it is the same moon I can see here in China—the China moon.

P. S. Please rename my chicken "China Moon," as a reminder to look at the moon.

Ida blew on the sheet of paper to dry the ink.

Then, with a self-conscious smile, she picked up the pen, dipped it once more, and signed her name in Chinese letters.

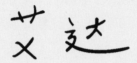

Chapter 5

Dance of the Dragon

MOLLIE PUSHED BACK THE HOOD of her thick, woolen cloak so she could see better in the dim chicken coop. She thrust cold fingers into first one nest, then another. One egg . . . two . . . three . . .

"Umph. Get off, Moon Chicken." She gave Ida's hen a shove off the warm nest. "Four . . ."

Ida. Didn't Ida say she was going to write every week? Hadn't they pledged to be pen pals forever? But here it was the end of January—two and a half *months* since they made that promise and exchanged locks of their hair—and nothing. No word. No letter.

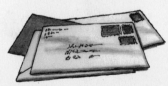

"Haven't I been writing every week?" she complained to Chicken Lottie, giving the reluctant hen a shove. "Well, since Christmas, anyway. But do I know where to mail it? No! . . . five," she added, putting Chicken Lottie's egg into her basket.

A few minutes later, Mollie trudged up the back stairs of Jones's Emporium to the family apartment. By the time she got chicken chores done after school, it was almost dark. Then she had to help with the baby while Mama got supper, and do her schoolwork . . . She hadn't even had a chance to look at the spring *Ladies Wear Catalog* that came last week.

She hung up her cloak with a big sigh and handed the egg basket to Mama. Mama took the basket with a sly smile. "Papa just brought up the mail. There." She pointed to some letters and advertisements on the kitchen table.

Mollie picked up the letters. The one on top had funny stamps in the corner. She sucked in her breath. The address read *Miss Mollie Jones, 19 Front Street* . . .

"Ida! A letter from Ida!" she screeched, clutching it to her chest.

"Open it!" laughed Mollie's mother. "What does she say?"

A staircase of curly heads and wide eyes popped into the warm kitchen and clustered around their big sister as Mollie carefully opened the sealed letter.

" 'Union Pacific Railroad, November 17,' " she read at the top. Why, Ida had started this letter only a few days after the Bakers had left Sugar Grove!

She read the entire letter out loud to her mother

and younger siblings—skipping the part about her secret crush on George Meriweather—and then again at the supper table for her father and Tom.

"Sounds like she mailed it the day after Christmas," said Mrs. Jones as she fed baby Mary spoonfuls of mashed potatoes. "My, my. Took that letter five weeks to get here."

"Ohhh . . . sailing on the *Empress of China*," sighed Janice dreamily. "Isn't that romantic?"

"I'd like to ride in one of those shentze contraptions!" Tom declared. "Wouldn't make *me* seasick."

"Do Ida and her mama and papa *really* sleep on top of a brick oven?" asked Bonnie with a worried frown on her rosy face.

Mollie suddenly pushed her chair back from the kitchen table. " 'Scuse me," she mumbled and ran from the room.

In her bedroom she jerked open the bottom drawer of the chest she shared with her sisters, pulled out the box of stationery, and lifted the lid. There lay the letter she'd been writing to Ida. She took it out and scanned through the pages. . . . *Pears Soap in my Christmas stocking. At school today . . . utterly ruined my blue dress! . . . dog almost got the chickens again.*

Pressing her lips together, Mollie suddenly ripped the pages in half, then ripped them again and again and threw the pieces on the floor.

"Mollie! What*ever* are you doing!"

Mollie whirled. She had not heard her mother come into the girls' bedroom.

59

"Oh, Mama," she wailed. "I can't send that boring old letter to Ida! She's writing about trains crossing the prairie, and . . . and a scary Chinaman chasing her out of the ship's boiler room, and bouncing like a sack of potatoes from Chefoo to . . . to Tengchow strung between two mules. And what did I write her about?" She rolled her eyes. "The latest chicken-coop adventure! Oh my, what I found in my Christmas stocking! Who teased who at Sugar Grove School! It's all so . . . *dull*." And Mollie burst into tears.

Mollie felt her mother's arms go around her. "Oh, Mollie, Mollie," crooned Anna Jones, pulling her down onto the bed and offering the handkerchief she always kept in her apron pocket. "Don't you see? That's *exactly* what Ida wants you to write about! She's lonely; she's missing all the little things, the familiar things that say 'home' to her. She will *love* hearing about our Christmas Day—the Chinese don't celebrate Christmas, remember?—and how the chickens are doing and 'who teased who' at Sugar Grove School."

Mollie blew her nose on her mother's handkerchief. "You—*hic*—really think so?"

Mrs. Jones brushed a stray curl from Mollie's damp, freckled face. "Yes, I do. I really do."

Mollie sat on the bed, thinking, after her mother had left the room. If it really took five whole weeks for a letter to go between China and Virginia, even if she mailed a letter tomorrow, it would be almost March before Ida heard from her—more than three months since they'd said good-bye. Oh! What if Ida thought she'd forgotten about her already?

Picking up the stationery box from the floor where she'd dumped it, Mollie carefully drew out a new sheet of the creamy paper with her name elegantly printed across the top. She placed it on the stool she used as a desk, unscrewed the cap of the dark green ink bottle, dipped the matching green pen, and carefully wrote, "Dear Ida . . ."

Boinnng! Boom-boom! Boinnng!

Ida and her parents lifted their heads with their rice bowls and chopsticks halfway to their mouths. "The drums and gongs are getting closer," said Thomas Baker, putting down his bowl. "I think they're coming down our street."

Ida got up from the little table and followed her father into the tiny side room where she slept. The new missionary pastor of Sha-Ling Baptist Church unlatched the window and pulled the two halves open. Sure enough, by leaning over the wide window ledge, father and daughter could see the front of the New Year parade turning a corner and heading their way.

"How many nights is this going to go on?" Nellie Baker's voice behind them was high-pitched, trying to be heard over the drums.

"Last night and tonight is all, my dear. Mr. Dan said the Chinese New Year is a two-day event. Oh, Ida, look!" A brightly colored cloth dragon with a huge head was weaving and bobbing at the front of the parade as it came toward them down the cobblestone street. The dragon head was held high on a stick by a person walking at the front of the creature, while behind him a row of pantaloons and cloth slippers could be seen prancing beneath the snakelike body as the dancers carried the dragon along over their heads.

Pastor Baker chuckled. "Never saw a sight like this in Sugar Grove."

"I should hope not!" Ida's mother sounded annoyed. "Honestly, Thomas. Such a pagan celebration. Remember Mr. Dan telling us on Sunday what happened to him four years ago?"

"Yes . . . yes, a terrible thing," Ida's father admitted. "But he also said the Chinese New Year is a warm, happy family time. We must be careful to sort out the truly pagan from customs that are just 'different.' Don't forget, Nellie, we Americans have our favorite holidays, too—Independence Day, Thanksgiving, Christmas—"

Boinnng! Boom-boom! Boinnng! The parade was almost upon them.

"Thanksgiving! Christmas!" Nellie Baker practically had to shout to be heard. "How can you possibly compare them to this? Those are *Christian* holidays!"

"Ah, but Christian and non-Christian alike celebrate them. They have become secular holidays in many respects." Ida caught her father's wink. He was teasing his wife.

"Humph!" said Nellie Baker. "Well, I for one am going back to my dinner before it goes stone cold." She flounced out of the room.

Thomas Baker followed his wife but turned at the doorway. "Coming, pumpkin?"

"No, Daddy. I want to watch a little longer."

Ida drew back slightly from the open window as the dancers and drummers filled the night. Glowing red lanterns hung from the eaves of tile rooftops all up and down the street. Flashes of red and yellow streamers kept time to the drums. Shouting, laughing boys, bundled in padded coats and trousers, jumped up and down beside the prancing dragon, trying to touch its beard. Rickshaws and two-wheeled carts filled with women, girls, and young children trotted past, joining in the revelry.

But something above the noisy parade caught Ida's eye. Above the red-tiled roofs and swaying lanterns hung a tiny sliver of moon. Ida blinked in surprise. Last night was the "new moon," invisible to the eye. But tonight already the moon was peeking out from its shadow.

Ida reached up a hand, as though cupping the thin slice of moon in her palm. "Oh, Mollie," she whispered, homesickness tightening in her throat, "why haven't you written to me? Are you watching the China moon? Or have you forgotten me?"

Blinking back sudden tears that filled her eyes, Ida shut the windows and clicked the latch. Turning the oil lamp a little brighter, she got out paper and pen.

Dearest Mollie,

You are so far away. But writing to you lets me pretend that we are curled up on this kang together, talking and sharing secrets.

Today is the second day of the Chinese New Year. Each year is named for a different animal—Year of the Rat, Ox, Tiger, Rabbit, Dragon, Snake, Horse, Sheep, Monkey, Rooster, Dog, Pig. After twelve years the cycle starts all over again. Let's see—that means you and I were born in the Year of the Dragon! Tom turns twelve this year, so he was born in the Year of the Horse, and Janice was born in the Year of the Rooster. (That should be the other way around, the way Tom "crows" about everything!)

The New Year parade came right past my window! The dancing dragon was a sight to see. . . .

Ida dipped her pen and continued to describe the sights and sounds that had filled the streets of Sha-Ling for the past two nights, drawing little pictures along the edges of her paper. Then she looked up. The parade was gone—only the red lanterns dancing from the roofs still glowed cheerfully.

Then she remembered. Not *everything* was warm and happy during the New Year—not for a Chinese Christian. Ida shuddered. After Daddy's Sunday sermon at Dan Ho-Bang's house, they had invited the old man to share their Sunday dinner of mein noodles and vegetables in broth, rice cakes, and pickled eggs.

As they sipped strong tea, he had said in his short-hand English, *"It almost Chinese New Year. Four years ago, I just baby Christian. No longer worship ancestral tablets, but had not destroyed. My brother came to my house, very angry."*

Ida closed her eyes. The scene Mr. Dan had painted had been vivid. . . .

The pounding on the door was demanding. "Dan Ho-Bang! Come out!" yelled voices on the other side.

Dan Ho-Bang opened the door. "Honorable brother! What do you want? A happy New Year to you." The old man craned his neck at the small crowd. "And to you, honorable cousins."

"Enough!" snapped Dan Li-Ping. "Your servant girl told us that you no longer worship our ancestral tablets! What disrespect is this?"

Mr. Dan gave a brief nod. "It is true. I can no longer worship our respected ancestors. I am a Christian now. I worship only one true God."

"Blasphemy!" cried one of the cousins. "He dishonors our family!"

"Seize him!" cried another.

The angry relatives grabbed Dan Ho-Bang, tied his hands and feet behind him tightly with thin ropes, and strung him from a pole held by two strong men. Someone brought out Dan Ho-Bang's ancestral tablets where he could see them plainly. The pain in his arms was agonizing, but then the kicks and blows began. Mr. Dan squeezed his eyes shut and prayed silently.

"Will you say nothing?" screamed his brother. "Take that! ... and that! ... and that!"

Ida shuddered. She could almost feel the kicks. As Mr. Dan had finished his story, her mother had laid a tender hand on the old man's arm. "Oh, Mr. Dan! What did you do?"

"Do? I do nothing. Say nothing. I beaten very bad. But some of my relatives realize my belief strong and beg brother to stop. Other Christians come help me when relatives leave. Other Christians, too, suffering much from relatives. So Christians send for Miss Moon do something."

Pastor Baker had looked bewildered. "Miss Moon? But why?"

Mr. Dan shrugged. "American missionaries protected by treaty. Some Chinese Christians want same protection. But Miss Moon not accept protection, even for self. Say it make 'weak Christians'! She living in nearby P'ingtu then, come quickly herself."

"What . . . what did she do?" Ida's mother had asked weakly. Ida saw the fear in her mother's eyes.

"Christians all together in one house, much afraid, talking what to do. Many relatives outside, angry. Some have knives, swords. Miss Moon—" the smile had widened on old Mr. Dan's face—"she stand between angry crowd and house. Say, 'You want kill these Christians, must kill me first.'"

"She didn't!" Nellie Baker's face had gone white.

"One man say, 'All right. I kill!' But others in crowd much impressed with small woman's big courage. Took man away. No big trouble since then."

Ida sighed, remembering Mr. Dan's story. What courage it took to be a Christian in China! She dipped her pen and bent over her letter to tell Mollie about it.

Ida was still working on her letter when she

heard a knock at the door in the other room and her father's chair scraping as he got up. Suddenly her heart started to pound. Mr. Dan's trouble had started on a New Year's night with a knock at the door—

"Mr. Dan!" she heard her father say. "Mr. Yuan! Come in, come in. Ida . . . Nellie . . . we have visitors!"

Ida let out her breath, blew on her letter to dry the ink, and parted the curtain into the main room of their little house. Mr. Dan and Mr. Yuan were sitting on chairs Pastor Baker had offered them.

Mr. Dan smiled happily at Ida as she pulled up a long-legged stool close to the old man. "We come, share New Year's family custom with our new friends," he said, pulling a bright mandarin orange from his pocket. Mr. Yuan, near in age to Mr. Dan, nodded.

The Bakers watched curiously as Mr. Dan peeled the skin from the orange, then loosened the sections until it looked like an orange lily, floating on a lily pad.

"Chinese families eat mandarin orange at New Year to symbolize family—many segments under one skin." Mr. Dan began giving the tiny orange sections to each person around the table. "Now you come, Pastor Baker . . . Mrs. Baker . . . Missy Baker . . . from America, far away. But you love same God, same Jesus." He beamed. "We all one family under same skin!"

Ida thought she saw both her father's and mother's eyes glisten. Almost reverently they took the orange sections from Mr. Dan's outstretched hand and began to eat. Ida, too, put the fruit into her mouth and bit into it.

It was oh, so sweet.

Chapter 6

Spy!

TING-A-LING! TING-A-LING!

Ida raised her head from the Chinese letters she was drawing. The bell at the front gate of the little mission house in Sha-Ling jangled again.

"Go, Missy, go!" urged Mr. Chiang, brushing her gently away from the table as though she were a butterfly that had landed accidentally on his book. "Do not keep important guest waiting."

Ida was glad for the distraction. She'd been studying all day—first United States history, English grammar, and mathematics with her mother, then Chinese with Mr. Chiang. Her mother was off to the marketplace with Mrs. Chow, the cook, and her father

69

was out looking for a building to house the Sha-Ling church.

The small garden at the front of the house was full of spring flowers—purple verbena, crape myrtle, touch-me-nots, hollyhocks, and jasmine spilling over the wall. Ida took a big whiff of the lovely smells, then hurried to lift the bar that held the gate in place. As she swung it open, she saw a middle-aged Chinese woman being helped from her sedan chair by one of her chair bearers. The other chair bearer bowed to Ida and, with a sweep of his hand toward the lady, announced: "La Di Mu!"

Ida felt uncertain. Her parents weren't home, and no one in the Sha-Ling Baptist Church was named La Di Mu. What should she do?

"Aren't you going to invite me in, Ida?" said a familiar musical voice in English.

Ida's mouth fell open. "Miss Moon! Of course! I . . . I didn't recognize you at first. And when the man said your name was La Di Mu—oh!" Ida's face turned red. Lottie Moon . . . La Di Mu. Of course.

Lottie Moon just laughed and paid the chair bearers from a cloth purse she took out of the front of her long blue robe that fell to her knees, nearly hiding the loose black trousers underneath. They passed Mr. Chiang on his way out as they went in, and he and Miss Moon bowed and smiled at each other in greeting.

Ida quickly poured two cups of tea from the pot that had been keeping warm on the brick stove. "Oh, Miss Moon, I'm so glad—"

"Come, come now, child. Must we be so formal? You may call me Aunt Lottie, like the Pruitt children do."

Ida blushed again. "All right, Miss—um, Aunt Lottie. I'm just so happy to see you! It's—it's . . ." To Ida's dismay, her chin began to quiver and tears spilled over her cheeks.

"I know, child." Lottie Moon's voice was warm, soft. "You're lonely. Yes, I know it well."

Ida sniffed and brushed the tears away with the back of her hand. "You mean, you g-get lonely, too?"

"Oh my, yes. When I first came to China, my sister Edmonia was here, but . . . she didn't fare well in China and had to return home. Sallie Holmes, now, she and I were great companions—her young husband was killed by bandits before I arrived, just before their little son was born. Sallie was the one who introduced me to country work, going village to village to share the Gospel. Oh my, talk about culture shock! I was so green!" Lottie Moon laughed. "But . . . she sent her son home to get an education, and later followed him. Now, Mrs. Crawford—she taught me most everything I know about mission work! But her husband . . . hmm. A very difficult man. He left the Southern Baptist Mission to start his own mission, and of course, Mrs. Crawford went with him." Lottie Moon sighed. "And so it goes. It's hard to keep a friend . . . but speaking of friends, Ida, did you ever hear from your friend back in Sugar Grove, the one you've been writing so faithfully?"

"Oh yes!" Ida fished for a handkerchief and blew

her nose. "I got a letter in March—and another in April! Oh, Miss Moon—I mean Aunt Lottie—when I got that letter from Sugar Grove all the way here to Sha-Ling, I felt like I'd been *found*!"

Just then Ida's mother bustled in with Mrs. Chow, and not long after, Ida's father appeared. The Bakers were excited to have a guest, and everyone laughed and talked over Mrs. Chow's supper.

Thomas Baker finally laid down his chopsticks. "Miss Moon, I cannot tell you how grateful we are for the money you sent from your personal savings to help buy a building for the Sha-Ling church."

"Thomas, my good man, I do hope you are seeking Mr. Dan's and Mr. Yuan's advice about an appropriate building. Be sensitive to Chinese custom. Keep it simple, plain, one story only." Lottie Moon shook her head. "Poor Mr. Crawford. He meant well, but when he built the Monument Street Baptist Church in Tengchow many years ago, he built it American-style, with a steeple. But it towers over nearby homes, causing offense to the Chinese eye."

"I see," said Pastor Baker, nodding thoughtfully. "What I see is that I have much to learn here in China!"

Miss Moon smiled encouragingly. "Study the culture along with the language, Thomas, and you will do well. Now!" She looked from one member of the Baker family to the next. "Maybe you wonder why I am making this visit. Thomas, I would like to steal your wife and daughter for some country work! It has been several years since I was able to visit the villages surrounding Sha-Ling and P'ingtu. I need a companion—and it will be a good experience for Ida, too. Because you, my dear man, would cause a scandal if you preached to these village women. Women's work for women!" Lottie Moon winked at Ida, threw back her head, and laughed.

Ting-a-ling! The bell over the door of Jones's Emporium jingled. Mollie glanced up from the catalog spread on the counter as Mrs. Meriweather swept in.

"Good morning, Mollie!" said the president of the Women's Missionary Union. "I see you're working in the store now that school's out. Is your father off to Richmond again?"

Mollie felt irritated, but she wasn't sure why. "No, he's just down to the blacksmith. Horse threw a shoe. Can I help you with something?"

But Mrs. Meriweather seemed more interested in snooping than shopping. "Haven't seen you at Sunbeams recently. . . ." Her comment was more like a question.

Mollie lifted her chin. "I'm fourteen now, Mrs. Meriweather. I'll be going to Hollins Institute this fall."

"Boarding school already! My . . . young people grow up so fast these days. Still not used to my George going off to college in a few months." Mrs. Meriweather seemed to be studying her. "Have you thought of what you want to do after Hollins, Mollie?"

Mollie squirmed. Why was Mrs. Meriweather asking all these questions! She wondered what the woman's reaction would be if she said, *Why, marry your gorgeous son George, of course, except he doesn't*

know I'm alive. But it came out, "Um . . . uh, not really."

Mrs. Meriweather reached out and turned up the cover of the catalog Mollie had been looking at. "Hmm. *Mahler Brothers Fashion Catalog . . .*" Her eyes took in Mollie's crisp, striped dress. Mollie felt smug. The catalog dress she'd bought with her own money was a tad dressy for working in the store. Still, it felt good to be well dressed to meet customers—and she felt *very* grown-up wearing the ladies corset Mama had given her for her fourteenth birthday as promised.

"You have a certain . . . style, Mollie. Flair. Have you ever thought about studying fashion design? I hear Albemarle Female Institute has a good arts program. Along with a classic education, of course."

Mollie sucked in her breath. Fashion design. Of course! That was exactly what she wanted to do! After boarding school, she'd go to college at Albemarle Institute . . . and then maybe study in Paris! Or Vienna!

How ironic that it was Mrs. Meriweather who had to point out the obvious.

". . . hear from Ida?" Mrs. Meriweather was saying.

"Uh . . . oh yes! Got a letter just the other day. She and her mother have been touring the farming villages with Miss Moon the last two months." Mollie heard herself repeating Ida's letter about the throngs of curious women and children, gawking, touching, allowing no privacy, even when they were resting on a kang in one of the village homes, and how hard it was for Ida to get used to the smell of unwashed bodies and children with untreated sores and runny noses. But how eagerly the children learned their "catechisms" and "Jesus Loves Me" in Chinese. Even the men and boys hung around in the back of the crowds to listen to Miss Moon's words.

But Mollie's mind was already half writing a letter to Ida to tell her the news: She wanted to be a fashion designer!

What was Mrs. Meriweather saying? ". . . so inspiring! Mollie dear, would you come to the next meeting of the WMU and share your letters? It's the kind of firsthand report from the mission field most of us never hear."

Mollie shrugged and grinned. Of course she would. And it was only fitting. Wasn't she practically a woman now?

"Ida, I need you to go with me to Mrs. Chow's house. I know you're writing a letter to Mollie, but . . . her grandchildren all have a rash and—" Mrs. Baker threw up her hands helplessly. "I honestly don't know what Mrs. Chow expects me to do! I'm not a doctor or nurse." Ida's mother laughed wryly. "If I'd *known* I was going to be a missionary in China instead of a pastor's wife in Virginia, I'd have studied medicine! These people need medical help—the missionary families, too!"

Ida shrugged. "It's all right, Mama. I can work on this tomorrow." What did one more day matter? She hadn't heard from Mollie since last July, when she'd written about wanting to study fashion design. Now it was fall already. What was holding up the mail? Or was Mollie just not writing? Ida kept writing, but she didn't even know Mollie's new address at boarding school.

Oh, how she'd love to just run up the stairs to the Joneses' lively apartment over the store in Sugar Grove, hide away with Mollie in the girls' bedroom, and just talk and talk for hours.

But Ida spent the next few hours in Mrs. Chow's small brick house as her mother examined the rash that covered the chest and back of two little boys and a little girl. "Measles? Scarlet fever? Oh dear, I don't know," worried Mrs. Baker. But she and Ida gave the children cool baths with baking soda to soothe the rash and bring down their fevers, and told Mrs. Chow and her daughter-in-law to keep the children in a dim room and give them plenty of water to drink.

"We'll need to cook our own supper tonight," Ida's mother said as they arrived back at their own gate and unlatched it. "I told Mrs. Chow to stay home as long as she's needed—oh! Mr. Dan!"

The old man and Ida's father were standing in the garden, talking with grave faces.

"Nellie! Ida! I'm glad you're home. Mr. Dan has some serious news for us." Thomas Baker took his wife's basket and led his family inside. Ida tried to read her father's face. What could it be? But she was unprepared for Mr. Dan's news.

"*War!* With Japan!" gasped Mrs. Baker.

The old man nodded gravely. "Japanese ships parade on horizon to make people afraid. Many rowdy Chinese soldiers in Tengchow want foreigners to get out. Some even accuse . . . accuse Miss Moon of being spy."

"A spy! But that's ridiculous!" Now Pastor Baker was upset.

"You know. I know. But war make people suspicious, afraid. May be best for missionaries in Tengchow to stay home for a while—or even get out of city, come inland."

"Miss Moon can certainly come here!" said Pastor Baker. "We'll send word."

"Good, good," said Mr. Dan. Concern loomed behind his kind eyes. "But I have even bigger request from Mrs. Pruitt in Hwanghsien." The old man hesitated.

"Speak up, man," urged Ida's father. "We'll do what we can."

"Many Chinese soldiers wounded from Japanese guns. Mr. Pruitt going to army camp to help treat burned soldiers—"

"But—why? He's not a doctor, is he?" cried Mrs. Baker.

Mr. Dan shrugged. "No. Miss Moon say she want to start mission hospital, but no doctors or nurses. Mr. Pruitt just doing what he can. But Mrs. Pruitt alone in Hwanghsien trying to keep home and school going." The kindly gentleman looked at Ida. "She want to know if young missy here could come help her with children while Mr. Pruitt gone."

Ida's heartbeat quickened; she saw alarm leap into her mother's eyes. Hwanghsien was three days away by shentze . . . away from her parents . . . in a strange city . . . closer to the war. Yet it'd be fun to see the Pruitt children again. Maybe she could really help! It felt good to be needed.

Thomas Baker laid a hand on his wife's arm. "If Ida wants to, I think we should say yes. God brought us here to serve. Ida can serve, too."

Pruitt household, Hwanghsien
November 9, 1894

Dearest Mollie,

November! A year ago I couldn't imagine spending even a week in China; now it's been almost twelve months. I thought I was getting used to it—a little— but suddenly China is at war with Japan and everything's all disrupted. Chinese soldiers are every- where, but there's been no fighting here in Hwanghsien (thank God!) so it seems a bit unreal. Except Mr. Pruitt just came home from treating burns in an army camp. I don't know why so many soldiers suffered burns; he doesn't talk about it. Oh, Mollie, China needs doctors and nurses so badly! I never even thought about it back in Sugar Grove. Dr. MacGregor was always just there if anyone got croup or fever or a broken leg.

Lottie Moon wants to start a hospital someday. That's good, because she has a way of making things happen eventually, one way or another!

I wrote you a month ago about coming to Hwanghsien to help take care of the Pruitt children— Mrs. P. had to run the school single-handed while Mr. P. was gone—but I don't know if you got my letter. (I don't think any mail is getting through because of the war. The last letter I got from you was in July. By now you must be at boarding school, and I don't have your address! Guess I'll just send this to your parents in Sugar Grove—they'll know how to get it to you.)

But I think your idea of studying fashion design in college is wonderful! Oh, Mollie, it's perfect for you! (I wish you were here to design something for me. Mama had to let down all my dresses this fall, but that's not going to last long—they're too tight in the waist, too. Maybe I should follow Aunt Lottie's example and wear Chinese clothes! Some of the embroidered silk tunics the women wear are actually very beautiful.)

As for me . . . I've been thinking about something, but I haven't told anyone yet. I've loved taking care of the Pruitt children the past few weeks. Little Ida— Mrs. P. calls us "Little Ida" and "Big Ida" so we don't get mixed up—follows me around like a puppy dog and loves me to read stories! But I'm worried about little Ashley. He just doesn't seem "right." Mrs. P. keeps saying, "He's doing better today, don't you think?" But I keep thinking of Isaiah and baby Mary—how rosy and bright-eyed they always looked, and full of giggles. But Ashley's eyes are big and sober, with dark circles around them, and he's so thin and pale for a three-year-old. Mama and I think he needs a doctor's care . . .

which started me thinking about what I want to do when I grow up.

China needs doctors and nurses so badly—maybe I should study medicine! I could be a nurse, or even a doctor! (Aunt Lottie told me her sister Orianna is a doctor. She and her husband both.) So here's my big idea: Could you find out if Albemarle Female Institute has a nursing program? Then when I'm seventeen, I could come back to Virginia, and we could go to college to-gether!—you studying fashion design and me, medicine. Wouldn't that be wonderful? Oh, Mollie, please find out and write me back.

With love, Ida

P.S. Aunt Lottie is coming to P'ingtu for Christ-mas—she has a second mission house there—and wants the Pruitts and us to join her there. I can't wait! It's not safe for missionaries in Tengchow right now—the Japanese gunboats are shelling it, and the army thinks "La Di Mu" is a spy because she blends so well with the Chinese people.

P.P.S. Let me know if you get this letter!

Chapter 7

Schoolhouse Refuge

THANK YOU, GEORGE." Mollie tried to sound sophisticated and grown-up as the tall young man
hefted her satchel onto the wooden porch of Jones's
Emporium, then helped her down from the sleigh.

"Don't mention it." George Meriweather hopped
back in the sleigh and slapped the reins on the
horse's rump.

"Good-bye, Mrs. Meriweather! Thanks again for
the lift!" Mollie waved as the Meriweathers' horse
took off at a good clip. She watched them go, then
smacked her forehead. She couldn't *wait* to write Ida
and tell her that she'd ridden home
from the train station in
George Meriweather's sleigh!
She, a lowly first year in sec-

ondary school, and he, a college man!

Just then the front door of the Emporium was jerked open, clanging the bell wildly. "Mollie's home! Mollie's home!" The screeching voices were accompanied by wild hugs and much jumping up and down by Janice, Bonnie, and Beth, who came flying out of the store into the December air with no coats on.

"Shoo, shoo, inside!" Mollie laughed, and the four sisters all tried to squeeze through the door like an eight-legged clump.

"Mollie! What are you doing home already? Didn't you say to pick you up at three o'clock?" Haley Jones came out from behind the counter looking confused, like he'd just been asked something he ought to know—the date of his wedding anniversary—and he didn't know the answer.

"I know, Papa! I'm early." Mollie gave her father a peck on the cheek. "There was an earlier train, so a bunch of us girls took it. Didn't have time to let you know. But it worked out." Mollie tried to sound offhand. "Mrs. Meriweather was at the station to pick up George, so they gave me a ride home."

"Oh. That's good, then. Going to Virginia State, isn't he?" Papa picked up her satchel. "Well, go on upstairs. Your mother will be excited to see you."

Mollie ran up the back stairs, her little sisters fast on her heels. Christmas was a week away, and Mollie was so glad to be home from boarding school for the holiday. The afternoon was a happy flurry of chasing "baby" Mary, who was almost two and running on chubby legs, making sugar cookies with

Beth and Bonnie, and trouncing Tom three checker games in a row.

Oh! It was good to be home. If only Ida . . .

"Mama, did any letters come for me?" she asked at supper, plopping a gob of mashed potatoes on Isaiah's plate.

She glanced up and caught a look between her mother and father. But Mrs. Jones just shook her head. "No, dear. No letters."

"Well, now." Mr. Jones cleared his throat. "Uh, the newspaper said China and Japan are at war. That could explain—"

"War!" Six pairs of eyes widened and stared at their parents. "Is Ida in danger?" "Are the Bakers going to die?" "Are they going to fight?" Baby Mary just stirred her mashed potatoes with her finger, singing a little song to herself.

"Whoa." Haley Jones threw up his hands. "I'm sure the Bakers and Miss Moon and the other missionaries are all right. They are American citizens, and there are treaties protecting foreigners in China. But the war has probably made it difficult for mail to get through. That's all. Now . . . let's finish our supper."

Frustrated, Mollie swallowed a dozen questions. She knew Papa didn't want everyone to get worried, but he never let them *talk*. What were the papers saying about this war? No one in Virginia seemed the least concerned—at least, she hadn't heard anything about it at school. Was Ida really all right?

When evening chores were done and the little ones in bed, Mollie quietly pulled her wool cloak off its peg and stepped out the back door onto the landing above the back stairs. The December sky was brilliant, like black ice salted with stars. A half-moon lit up the winter's first snow, and the bare trees cast long shadows, like lacy patterns on a baby-blue blanket.

"Are you looking at the moon tonight, Ida?" she whispered. She felt a little guilty. She hadn't done much "moon watching" since she'd been away at school—so many new faces and friends to keep her busy. Did Ida look at the moon every night, wondering if Mollie was looking at it, too?

Ida stood shivering in the little walled garden in front of the Baker home in Sha-Ling, trying to catch a glimpse of the full moon as clouds scuttled across the night sky. She wished this cold she had would go away; sometimes it was so hard to catch her breath.

A short, shadowy form in a thick, padded coat appeared at her elbow but said nothing. Ida knew it was Aunt Lottie. The middle-aged missionary had a way of being a comfortable presence without having to fill the silence with lots of talk.

It was Ida who broke the stillness of the January night, her voice wheezing a little. "Do you really have to go back to Tengchow tomorrow, Aunt Lottie?"

"Oh my, yes, child. I came to P'ingtu and Sha-Ling to spend Christmas, but it's now the middle of January! My excuses have run out." Miss Moon chuckled.

The full moon broke through the clouds and filled the garden with its silvery light. The rooftops of Sha-Ling beyond the walls leaped into view, like sentries around a castle.

"I've been talking to your parents, Ida," said Miss Moon. "Anna Pruitt would like you to come with me as far as Hwanghsien. You were so helpful to her a couple months ago—she hardly knows how to manage without you! Ashley is not well, you know, and needs lots of attention; but they've also got a school to keep running. A big plus is that you could also attend classes in the mission school. You might learn Chinese faster along with other girls your age."

Ida felt the familiar tug between excitement and uncertainty. It got very lonely here in Sha-Ling. At least at the Pruitts she was in a household of children, and many of the Chinese schoolgirls were in and out of the house. But . . . should she leave her parents again so soon? Would they feel abandoned? Of course, if they were home in Sugar Grove, she'd be away at boarding school, just like Mollie.

She found her voice. "What did my parents say?"

"That it was up to you."

Riding with Lottie Moon in the rocking shentze was an education in itself. Wrapped warmly in thick, padded blankets, Ida listened in fascination as the missionary told stories of her girlhood growing up at Viewmont, the Moon family plantation in Albemarle

County. "You went to Hollins Institute when you were my age?" Ida cried in delight. "But that's where Mollie is going to school!"

"Hmm. I hope she is behaving herself better than I did," snorted Miss Moon. "At your age I thought I was too clever for religion, even though I had been raised in a solid, churchgoing, Baptist family. But my father had just died in a boating accident . . . guess I was trying to find my own way." Miss Moon's eyebrows arched. "Didn't find my way, though, until I gave my life to Jesus my first year of college."

The stories went on . . . how Lottie and her mother barely held Viewmont together during the Civil War—

"You hid your silver in a field and never found it again?" gasped Ida.

Miss Moon chuckled. "Mm-hmm. How's that for scatterbrained? We heard the Union soldiers were advancing, so I took the silver and hid it. Hid it good. So good we never found it again." Her chuckle turned into a guffaw and soon had Ida laughing so hard she was gasping for breath.

Ida glanced out the front of the shentze and suddenly her laughter died. "Aunt Lottie, look!" The road outside Hwanghsien seemed much more crowded than usual. They passed old men pushing carts full of belongings, fathers carrying big bundles on their backs, women stumbling along on bound feet, their cloth shoes soaking wet in the slush, and shivering children clinging to their trouser legs—all going the other way out of the town.

"*Ting!* Stop!" Miss Moon called out to the mule

driver. She pointed to the stream of people heading south and sent off the mule driver with a wave of her hand. In a few moments he was back, speaking rapid Chinese with Lottie Moon.

Ida's heart pounded. What was going on?

Miss Moon finally crawled back under the bulky blankets inside the shentze. "The Japanese are bombarding Tengchow," she told Ida. "Many people are fleeing the city. Hwanghsien is already full of refugees, so these people are heading farther south." Suddenly she sat bolt upright. "I must get to Tengchow as quickly as possible."

"*What?* But Japanese gunships are shelling the city!" Mr. Pruitt was as shocked as Ida had been when Miss Moon made her announcement.

"But I must find out what has happened to the Hartwells and the other missionaries—I cannot simply abandon them." Lottie Moon had obviously made up her mind and would not be deterred. "Ida, take care of that cough . . . I will send word as soon as I can."

The Pruitts and Ida watched as the mule driver headed north toward Tengchow with Miss Moon's hired shentze. A small seed of fear threatened to sprout inside Ida. Then she felt Little Ida's hand slip into hers. "I'm glad you've come," whispered the little girl, smiling up at her.

Not a day went past but Chinese Christians from Tengchow showed up at the Hwanghsien mission. None of them had seen or heard any word of Lottie Moon. Only one man had anything to tell, with much headshaking. "House of La Di Mu ... big hole in garden wall, hole in house ..."

Ida was alarmed. Not Little Cross Roads! Such a beautiful little house ... and what about Aunt Lottie? Was she all right? The Pruitts must have been concerned, too, because Mr. Pruitt announced daily prayer meetings until the crisis was over.

Soon the Hwanghsien mission was full of refugees fleeing Tengchow, camping out in the schoolrooms as best they could. Mr. and Mrs. Pruitt bravely held classes for the boys and girls in separate rooms in the mornings. In the evening the Hwanghsien church members crowded into the already crowded schoolrooms for daily prayer.

Ida knew she'd be busier in Hwanghsien than she was in Sha-Ling, but she hadn't quite imagined *this*. Big pots of vegetables, noodles, and rice simmered all day on the brick stove in the schoolhouse to help feed the refugees. Ida not only had to keep Little Ida and Ashley out from underfoot, but she trekked to the common well three times a day to lug home buckets of water for washing and cooking. Fires had to be kept burning in the brick stoves not only to cook the food but to heat the sleeping kangs against the winter's damp chill. Sometimes she helped Mrs. Pruitt visit the homeless families crowded into the schoolrooms, giving flour boiled in milk to children

with the runs, spoonfuls of horseradish-root-and-sugar syrup for colds, and soap, water, and clean rags for cuts, scrapes, and wounds suffered in the exodus from Tengchow.

Ida's wheezing cough lingered on, even though

she tried to hide it from Mrs. Pruitt. Some days it was not so bad; other days it seemed worse. The scariest part was when she felt like she'd swallowed cotton and couldn't breathe. But quite by accident she discovered that the steam from the big cooking pots seemed to help. After that she often hung around the steamy kitchen, offering to help. Mrs. Pruitt said, "Why, thank you, Ida," but gave her a funny look.

And then the letter arrived.

For a brief second Ida's heart leaped. A letter from Mollie? But the messenger wasn't the regular man who delivered mail. And everyone knew overseas mail wasn't getting through. Who could it—

"Praise God, it's from Miss Moon!" cried Mr. Pruitt, recognizing the beautiful script. "Here, Anna, read it."

Ida gathered Little Ida and Ashley into her lap as Anna Pruitt opened the folded paper. Several of the Tengchow Christians crowded into the already small kitchen. They all seemed to be holding their breath as she read aloud.

Little Cross Roads, Tengchow
February 4, 1895

Mr. and Mrs. C. W. Pruitt,
My dear brother and sister—first of all, rest assured that I am alive and well! But the situation here in Tengchow is quite chaotic. I had a shock when I first arrived at Little Cross Roads, for a shell had blown a big hole in my garden wall, and the veranda and doorway have both been damaged. But that was a small thing compared to not being able to find any of my fellow

missionaries. They were simply gone!

I was afraid they'd been arrested, but a passerby who saw me knocking on Hartwells' door said they'd been rescued by an American ship! It seems the USS Yorktown bullied its way through the Japanese blockade and sent a ship's boat to shore to rescue any American citizens. Japanese shells were falling all over the city, so Mr. and Mrs. Hartwell and the other missionaries had to make their way down some icy cliffs to get to the boat. In the confusion, all of the Hartwells' luggage got left on the shore, and has since disappeared.

I guess I just missed getting "rescued," but since I have no desire to leave China, it is just as well! However, it seemed pointless to stay in Tengchow, so I tried to find a mule driver to take me back to P'ingtu, but I could not hire one for any price! It was every man for himself.

I was sitting in my damaged house, pondering what I should do, when several of the upper-class women in the city came knocking on my door. I was surprised to see them, for these women and their husbands had always ignored me and the other missionaries. But now they were begging me to stay to help calm the people. I could not refuse! God brings us opportunities to be His light when we least expect it.

The terror of the people is quite real. The shelling goes on from the Japanese ships every day, and Chinese guns are quite ineffective. I quell my own fear by reminding myself that I am immortal until my work for God is done.

Give my love to all the children in the school, and of course Ida, Little Ida, and Ashley, too.

With warmest regards,
Lottie Moon

A murmur went around the little crowd of refugees in the kitchen, most of whom knew Miss Moon in Tengchow, as Mr. Pruitt translated what the letter said. "We must thank God for her safety—and continue to pray," Mr. Pruitt added soberly. "The danger is not over yet."

Lottie Moon's words echoed in Ida's head as she led Little Ida and Ashley away to get washed up for supper. *"I am immortal until my work for God is done."* What did Aunt Lottie mean? That nothing could happen to her as long as God still had work for her to do?

Ida thought of all the times she felt frightened in this strange land. Why was she such a scaredy-cat? Maybe God had work for *her* to do . . . here in China. The idea about becoming a nurse often played in her mind. . . . Was *that* what God wanted her to do?

She felt strangely comforted.

Chapter 8

Thief on the Wall

THE WAR WAS OVER.

Once again the roads were full of refugees, this time returning to Tengchow, hoping they would find their homes still standing. The Japanese ships were gone. The damp chill of winter had given way to the warm breezes of spring and summer, and farmers wearing wide, straw sun hats were once again in their fields, guiding the plows behind big, gentle oxen that waded *glop, glop, glop* through the muddy earth.

As much as she loved Little Ida and Ashley Pruitt, Ida was glad to head home to Sha-Ling. Home. Funny, she'd never thought the little mission house with its pantry-like sleeping kang would ever be "home." But she was tired from the months of backbreaking work at the Hwanghsien mission, and she still had bouts of coughing at night when it was hard to breathe. She hated to admit it—especially since her fifteenth birthday was coming up in June—but she wanted her mother.

As Ida walked into the little walled garden, a riot of blue, pink, and yellow flowers welcomed her home. She was so excited to see old Mr. Dan and Mrs. Chow that she gave them both big hugs, setting off a flurry of big smiles and bows bobbing up and down. At suppertime, she hungrily scooped mouthfuls of Mrs. Chow's best dish of chicken and noodles with her chopsticks, trying to answer her parents' endless questions between bites. But Ida also noticed that her parents talked about their own struggles and victories of the past few months . . . almost as if she were a grown-up.

"Even though the war was with the Japanese," said her father, "people here in Sha-Ling seemed suspicious of anyone foreign—"

"Oh yes!" Ida's mother winced. "Every time I left the house, children yelled, 'Zou kai! Go away, foreign devil!' Sometimes when I went into a shop, the shopkeeper would turn his back and ignore me."

"Not our church members, of course," Thomas Baker added hastily. "They have steadfastly been our friends. But now that the war is over, suddenly people are stopping to listen when Mr. Dan and I preach in the street and are openly discussing the Bible."

Ida's mother beamed. "Mr. Dan says we have new

esteem because we stayed here with our church people instead of running off to the American consulate in Chefoo."

"Same with Aunt Lottie!" Ida exclaimed. She told her parents about Lottie Moon's letters, how she was the only missionary who stayed in Tengchow during the Japanese bombardment. The wealthy people who had ignored her before now showed respect.

"Speaking of letters," said Mrs. Baker, "you got three all at once from Mollie last week! They're in my sewing bas—"

Ida flew from the kitchen into her parents' sleeping room and snatched the letters from the basket before her mother finished. Three letters! The mail was getting through at last! A few moments later she was sitting on the wide window ledge in her little pantry, trying to figure out which letter came first. One was written last fall at school, another at Christmas, another back at school. Her eyes flew over the pages like a smorgasbord feast, tasting a little bit here, a little bit there. . . .

> . . . My rommate's name is Sarah Michaels. She's all right, I guess, but has NO sense of humor! Last night when the matron was in a meeting, a couple of the first-year girls and I snuck in and short-sheeted her bed. I asked Sarah if she wanted to join in the fun, and she looked like I'd asked her to rob a bank! If Miss Pendergrass discovers who did it, I'm going to know who told!

> . . . Did you get my letter about what Mrs. Meriweather said—about me studying fashion design? You must not, or I would have heard . . .

Ida groaned. She *did* get Mollie's letter, and she *did* answer! But if the mail hadn't been getting through since last fall—

Suddenly she felt the familiar tightness in her chest, like rubber bands cutting off her airways. She grabbed her nightgown and tried to muffle the coughing fit that always resulted from her efforts to get her breath. Why *wouldn't* this cough go away? When the spell passed, she wiped her eyes with the soft flannel nightgown and picked up the letters again.

> . . . *Papa told me he read in the newspapers that there's a war going on in China. Oh, Ida, I'm so scared. Please, please, please be all right. I looked at the moon tonight and tried to imagine it watching over you.*

> . . . *I'm jealous of your Pruitt family. You have a new family to love you! Don't forget the Joneses back here in Sugar Grove love you, too.*

> . . . *Didn't see anything of George Meriweather during Christmas vacation—except for the ride from the station he and his mother gave me. Woe. I know he thinks I'm just a lowly toad. Now I'm back at school for second term, which is mostly just hard work.*

Ida finished the three letters and smiled. Maybe Mollie was reading a pile of *her* letters that had just arrived. As she hid them away in the chest of drawers, she became conscious of her mother's low voice in the other room. ". . . that cough of hers. Oh, Thomas, you don't think she has consumption, do you?"

Goosebumps prickled the back of Ida's neck. Consumption? What was that?

❖ ❖ ❖ ❖

"Ida? This is Dr. Randle."

Ida struggled to sit up against the pillows that littered the sleeping kang. She was so *tired*. Breathing was such a struggle. But she gave a little smile to Dr. Randle. He looked English, middle-aged, with a neat moustache and serious eyes. It was a pleasant face.

"Dr. Randle is helping Miss Moon make plans for a hospital in Shantung Province," said Ida's father. "But right now he's making the rounds of the mission stations to give medical checkups to missionary families. He just came from Hwanghsien."

Ida tried to suck in a breath. "How's Ashley Pruitt?" she wheezed.

The corners of Dr. Randle's mouth curved. "A plucky lad! He's holding his own, though his resistance is low." The accent was definitely English. "But your parents tell me you've been having a troubling cough since last Christmas . . . trouble breathing. I would like to examine you. You're fifteen? Just had a birthday?"

Ida rolled her eyes as the doctor placed a stethoscope to her chest. "Some birthday," she croaked. "I was sick as a dog. Spent my birthday with my head over a pot of steaming water just so I could breathe."

"Mmm-hmm." The tiny room fell silent as the doctor listened to Ida's chest. He checked her ears and tongue and throat. He listened to her chest again.

Finally he stood back and frowned. "I don't think it's consumption. Sounds more like asthma . . . but I can't be sure. I'd have to observe her for a while." He looked at Ida's anxious parents. "I'm heading back to Tengchow in a couple days and will be there for several months. What I'd *like* to do is take Ida back with me, have her stay with Miss Moon for a while. That way I can observe her, treat her if necessary." The doctor looked almost apologetic. "I know that's a difficult choice, but Ida is a very sick girl. And there's no doctor this far from Tengchow . . . not yet."

Tears sprang to Ida's eyes, and she turned her head to the wall. She only just got home! She didn't *want* to leave her parents again so soon—not when she felt so miserable.

But later, as she listened to Dr. Randle talking to her parents, two hopeful sparks brightened the thought of another long trip by shentze. If she had to go stay somewhere, Little Cross Roads was the coziest place in the world she could think of. And second, maybe she could talk to Dr. Randle about her idea of becoming a nurse.

Lottie Moon sliced a lemon and squeezed the tart juice into Ida's tea. "When my throat is bothering me, this always seems to help." She gave Ida a firm "Drink it!" look.

Ida swallowed. The hot, sour liquid did feel good. "You have trouble with your throat, too, Aunt Lottie?" Ida made a mental note to remember "tea with lemon" when she became a nurse.

Miss Moon grinned impishly. "Yes, but it's only because I talk too much!"

Ida started to protest, but her hostess held up her hand. "No, no, I mean it's the country work. When I'm visiting the villages, I end up talking to people from dawn to dusk—and then some! But lately my voice has been giving out, and I have to nurse my throat back to health before I can—" Miss Moon stopped suddenly and jerked her head up, listening. Then, quick as a cat, she darted out of the room. A moment later Ida heard her voice rise shrilly, rattling off a string of Chinese. It almost sounded like a scuffle, and Ida was just about to go see what was happening when Miss Moon reappeared, shaking her head.

"What happened?" Ida cried.

"Hmph. Fuss and bother. Thief in the storeroom—third time this month!" Lottie Moon lowered her solid frame into a chair near the kang where Ida was resting. "It's the war. Been in China over twenty years, and nothing like this has ever happened. But the war has brought out the best and worst in people. Some people don't care what their neighbors think if they are seen talking to the 'foreign devil'! But there are a few who would like to see all foreigners thrown out of China—they call themselves Boxers, but don't ask me why! I think they encourage common thieves to harass us." She threw up her hands. "Not that there's much to take! I don't think it's wise to keep expensive things around." She winked at Ida. "There's more than one good reason to live simply!

People with too much stuff attract people who want to steal it."

Ida thought about this when Lottie went off to a meeting of the Tengchow Baptist board that evening. She lit a candle to hold back the twilight, found the letter she'd been writing to Mollie, and scratched away with her pen and ink.

> . . . *The funny thing is, Mollie, Miss Moon is one of the most generous people I know! Beggars have come to the gate nearly every day since I've been here at Little Cross Roads, and she always gives them a few coins or something to eat. No one gets turned away. Surely people must know this. So why—*

A noise outside startled Ida, and a drop of ink smudged the letter. She listened. There it was again . . . a scraping noise close by. She tried to swallow the flutter of panic that rose in her throat. Maybe it was just Aunt Lottie coming home—or a peddler pushing his wheelbarrow down the street.

No, the sound came from *this* side of the garden wall.

Quickly Ida blew out the candle and stole quietly to one of the windows along the veranda of Little Cross Roads. The August moon was in its last quarter, softly lighting the courtyard. At first she saw nothing. Then she saw the branches of the chinaberry tree shaking in a funny way, only on one side. It took her a few seconds to realize there was someone *in* the tree . . . someone who had climbed over

the top of the wall, jumped into the tree, and was now climbing down into the garden.

Ida's breath came short and fast. Suddenly she was sucking in more breath than she was able to expel, and the familiar bands tightened across her chest. This wasn't just fear; she was having an asthma attack!

Gathering her courage and all the strength she could muster, Ida yelled out in Chinese, "Stop, thief! We see you! Help, someone, help!"

The noisy chatter in the dining room of Hollins Institute settled into whispers and a few leftover giggles as the school matron tapped a glass for attention. Everyone looked forward to mail call.

"Laura Blackwood . . . Celia Thorndike . . . Mollie Jones . . . is Mollie here?"

"Mollie!" hissed the girl sitting next to Mollie. "Miss Pendergrass called your name. You got a letter!"

Mollie jumped. She'd been thinking about the little flared caps off the shoulders of Evangeline Shepherd's new maroon dress. The girls at Hollins wore the uniform of white shirtwaist and navy blue skirt every day except Sunday, and on that day there was much whispering and comparing of whose dress was the most recent fashion, even when they were supposed to be paying attention during the sermon at Enon Baptist Church across the road. Were those little flares the newest fashion, Mollie wondered, or just something Evangeline's mother added?

"Who's it from?" Three curious friends crowded around Mollie as she returned to the table with her letter. "Look at those foreign stamps!" "Is it your friend in China?" "Oh, what does she say!" "Open it, Mollie!"

But Mollie waited until she was back in her dormitory room before she slowly loosened the seal and opened the folded pages. Why did she feel so hesitant? Wasn't she *glad* to get a letter from Ida? Well, of course she was, but . . . sometimes reading Ida's letters made her uncomfortable. It wasn't anything Ida *said* exactly . . . it was just that they seemed to live in two separate worlds.

She was almost done reading when a shadow fell across the letter. "How long ago did she send it?" asked a quiet voice. It was Sarah Michaels, Mollie's roommate.

Mollie looked up. "It's dated August 24 . . . almost two months ago." A couple of her other friends had followed Sarah into the room.

"Isn't she the one who has consumption?" said Evangeline. "What is consumption, anyway?"

"Like tuberculosis, I think," said Sarah. "I heard it's very contagious."

Mollie felt defensive. "No, now they think it's asthma," she said, waving the letter. "That's different." At least she hoped it was. Mollie didn't want to admit she didn't know anything about asthma.

"Asthma! My aunt has that." A third girl joined the conversation. "Auntie's allergic to everything— feathers, milk, dust, you name it. Gets so bad she can't breathe!"

Mollie nodded. "Ida's having trouble like that."

"Mollie, would you read us your friend's letter— like you did last time?" Sarah asked. She sounded genuinely interested. "It's so *romantic* to think of a girl—just like us—writing all the way from China."

Mollie hesitated, then shrugged. Why not? After all, *she* was the one with the friend in China. It gave her a certain . . . status.

A growing knot of girls clustered around Mollie's bed as she read Ida's letter out loud. When she was done, the girls all talked at once.

"Thieves! Breaking into the missionary's house while she's right there?"

"We don't even lock our doors in *our* town."

"Boxers . . . they sound scary. What do you think their name means?"

"Did Ida really chase off that thief . . . in Chinese?" Sarah's voice was full of admiration.

"Good thing that English doctor was walking Miss Moon home, or she might've *died*."

"Pooh. You can't die from asthma."

"Sure you can!"

"She wants to be a nurse? Mollie, does that mean she's thinking of *staying* in China? I thought you said she didn't want to go in the first place!"

"Can't she make her own decision when she's grown? I mean, she doesn't have to stay in China just because her parents are missionaries, does she?"

"Do you think she'll come back home to go to college?"

The buzz of voices swirled all around Mollie. Good questions! As soon as the matron rang the bell for study time, she was going to write Ida and ask a few of those questions herself.

Chapter 9

Laughing Out Loud

IDA TRIED TO KEEP HER BALANCE on the small, three-legged stool. How long was it going to take Aunt Lottie to pin these trousers? She glanced down at the shapeless cotton legs. "But I'll look like a boy!" she protested.

"Nonsense." Lottie Moon's reply was muffled by the pins in her mouth. She took them out one by one and stuck them firmly into the cloth, narrowing the waist. "With a face and hair like yours? Humph. You could wear a burlap sack and *still* look like a girl."

Ida reddened. She wasn't fishing for compliments. "I . . . I just mean it feels so strange to wear these Chinese clothes."

"You'll get used to it. There." Miss Moon got stiffly to her feet. "That'll have to do until we can have some new ones made. But face it, Ida Baker, you have grown right out of your dresses! If your mother wants to make you some American-style dresses, that's up to her. But sewing is not my strong point, and besides, you've been in China over two years! Isn't it time you quit dressing like a *foreigner*?" There was a hint of teasing in the throaty voice.

Ida decided not to answer. It wasn't that she minded the idea of dressing in Chinese clothes so much. Her new friend, Mai-Ling, always looked beautiful in her embroidered silk tops and swishy trousers. But Aunt Lottie's made-over boxy tops and trousers just didn't have the same effect.

Ida took off the plain cotton top and trousers, which were pinned inside out, ready to sew up with needle and thread. She giggled. If *Mollie* saw her dressed like this, she would absolutely *die*.

A sudden wave of homesickness swept over her. Not only for Mollie and Sugar Grove, but for her parents. She'd been at Little Cross Roads for six months under Dr. Randle's care, and had only seen her parents once in that time—when Papa had to come to Tengchow on mission business. Christmas and the Chinese New Year had come and gone. But at least Dr. Randle said she was doing lots better and could look forward to spending the summer in Sha-Ling.

Which was great, except . . . now she had a friend

here in Tengchow! Mai-Ling was just a year older than Ida and was being tutored in English by Lottie Moon. The missionary got the bright idea that Mai-Ling could also help Ida with her Chinese.

Both girls were shy at first, but soon were giggling at their clumsy attempts to speak the other's language. Ida admired the beautiful embroidered handiwork on Mai-Ling's tunics, and Mai-Ling offered to teach her—begging Ida, in turn, to teach her to draw. Soon Mai-Ling was spending more and more time at Little Cross Roads after her lessons, and the two girls ended up talking and cooking and eating and laughing, just like Ida and Mollie used to do.

Ting-a-ling! Ting-a-ling! Ida's thoughts were interrupted by the bell at the gate. Oh! She had to get these ugly clothes off. A few moments later she heard Mai-Ling's musical voice and Lottie Moon's throaty laugh, and then another strange voice, this one male. Then Miss Moon stuck her head in the doorway of Ida's sleeping room. "Mai-Ling is here for her English lesson, but I have another visitor who wants to speak to me. Maybe she can give you a hand sewing up those trousers until I'm finished."

Ida rolled her eyes. There was no hiding the ugly things now. But as the two girls got Miss Moon's sewing basket and worked side by side in a corner of the kitchen, she had to admit it was more pleasant to do mending with company. In the next room, she could hear low voices as Miss Moon talked to her visitor. But Ida noticed that Mai-

Ling was quieter than usual.

"Are you well, Mai-Ling?" she asked in Chinese.

Mai-Ling nodded, her eyes cast down. Her skin was a lovely light color, with just a touch of red on her cheeks and lips, and her sleek black hair was swept into a knot at the back of her head.

"What is it?" Ida pressed. Mai-Ling was usually so sunny.

"I . . . I am to be married at the next full moon."

Ida was shocked. "*Married!* But . . . I didn't even know you were engaged!"

Mai-Ling gave a half smile. "I am betrothed since I was twelve. To important family here in Tengchow. But . . . I have never seen my husband-to-be. He has been overseas in English university. That is why I must . . . why I come here to learn English, so I can be a good wife of Chinese official."

Ida was still dumbfounded. She was going to be sixteen in June, but even if she was seventeen, like Mai-Ling, she couldn't *imagine* getting married to someone she'd never met!

"Aren't you even a *little* bit excited?"

Mai-Ling shrugged. "Curious, maybe. But mostly . . ." Mai-Ling swallowed. "Ever since I come to La Di Mu's house, I not only learn English, but about God's Son, Jesus. So good! I am so happy!" The familiar sunny smile lit up Mai-Ling's face. Then the cloud passed over again. "But husband's family not Christian. Must worship ancestor's graves during marriage ceremony. If I defy this custom, new mother-in-law may beat me for being rebellious wife."

Mai-Ling's lip quivered, and tears welled up in her eyes. But the Chinese girl quickly blinked them away, and she held her head up. "But I cannot worship ancestors. Not now, since I know about Jesus."

Ida was astonished. If she *knew* she'd get a beating for being a Christian, what would she do? Up till now, being a Christian had always seemed so . . . easy. She'd grown up in a pastor's family. As far back as she could remember, she'd heard about Jesus. When she was four years old, her mother had helped her pray a prayer asking Jesus to live in her heart. Almost everyone she knew in Sugar Grove went to church and called themselves a Christian—even though some of them were Presbyterians or Methodists, which wasn't *quite* the same as being a good Southern Baptist, though she wasn't sure exactly why.

"You . . . you must talk to Aunt Lottie," Ida urged her friend. "She'll be done—"

Just then the girls heard laughter coming from the next room. It was the young man talking to Miss Moon. Ida felt irritated. Here was Mai-Ling in the kitchen, about to get married to a complete stranger, probably going to get a beating on her wedding day because she'd become a Christian and didn't want to worship the ancestors anymore, and Miss Moon's guest was just—

"I can't help it!" came the young man's voice gleefully. "I can't help believing! You tell me such wonderful news!" Peals of laughter seemed to bounce off the walls of Little Cross Roads.

Mai-Ling and Ida looked at each other, then stole

to the doorway and peeked in. The young man was on his feet, jumping up and down, then slapping his thigh and doubling over with laughter. "Oh! Oh! It's so wonderful!"

Ida caught Aunt Lottie's eye. Was the young man crazy? But Miss Moon just gave the two girls a broad smile and said in English, "All I did was tell him about Jesus!"

Mollie Jones took a corner of her apron and mopped her face. The heat inside Jones's Emporium prickled her skin, like wearing a thick wool sock. Too hot for June. Must be too hot for customers, too, because the store had been empty for the past hour.

She blew a damp curl from her forehead, went into the back room, and pumped a glass of water to drink from the sink pump. Then she settled back on the stool behind the counter and reached into her apron pocket for Ida's letter that had come that morning. Papa wouldn't mind if she finished it, as long as there weren't any customers to help.

She skimmed through the first part of the letter. Where did she leave off reading? Oh, here . . .

> *. . . Mai-Ling decided to get baptized before her wedding. I thought it was terribly brave of her. Now everyone will know she has become a Christian! I think I might have wanted to keep it a secret for a while, till I'd met my new husband and found out whether he was a kind man or an ogre! But, oh, Mollie, a person must be very brave to become a Christian in China! Their families can get very angry. It has really made me think about whether I am willing to suffer for what I believe.*

Mollie squirmed on the wooden stool. Suffer?

What was Ida talking about? Pagan Chinese customs were one thing—no wonder that poor bride was afraid. But Ida? Why would Ida suffer? She had her whole life ahead of her! She should be thinking about . . . about her education, and becoming a grown woman, and meeting a nice young man. Didn't Ida use to say she just wanted to get married and raise a nice big family? Really, China must be a very depressing place. It would be *so good* for Ida to get away and come back to America for college. The next time she wrote she was going to push very hard.

Her eyes picked up the letter again.

The night before Mai-Ling's wedding—she still had not met her groom—the whole Tengchow Baptist Church met to pray. The young man who had burst out laughing for joy when he heard about Jesus—this time he was weeping for Mai-Ling. He was so afraid for her, because he knew what could happen to her. To not worship the family's ancestors would seem so disrespectful to the mother-in-law, it would be like a scandal and bring shame on the family. But Mai-Ling herself seemed so peaceful—not like the day when she first told me. Everyone prayed for her, and then the rickshaw came to get her, and after she left to go to the wedding, the church continued to pray.

We didn't hear anything for a week or two. Mollie, I felt so lonely again. Mai-Ling was the only friend near my age that I've had since I've been in China. And now she was gone. But then one day she came to Little Cross Roads, and her face was full of joy. "What happened!" we asked. She said the first time she talked to her new husband-to-be, she told him very respectfully about her new faith, and that she couldn't worship at his ancestors' graves. But she said she respected his family and his ancestors and wanted to be a good wife. The man must be a good fellow, because he spoke to his mother and said his new bride did not have to do that part of the ceremony!

I was so amazed. We prayed . . . and God answered!

A small jealous thought wormed its way into Mollie's mind. Mai-Ling this, Mai-Ling that—Ida's whole letter had been about Mai-Ling! Was Mai-Ling Ida's new best friend? Had Ida forgotten that she and Mollie were soul sisters? Best friends forever?

"Why the big frown?" said a pleasant male voice.

Startled, Mollie nearly fell off the stool. George Meriweather was standing on the other side of the counter. Where had *he* come from!

"Oh!" she said. She wasn't blushing, was she? "Oh, just reading a letter." She waved Ida's letter to document her statement. "Uh, can I help you? Would you like something?"

But George craned his neck to see the letter in Mollie's hand. "Good little drawings—is that from Ida Baker?"

The small jealous worm puffed itself a little larger. She didn't especially want George Meriweather to be giving compliments to Ida. She nodded and started to put the letter away, but George put out his hand and touched her arm.

"No, wait, I'd really like to hear Ida's letter . . . if it's not too personal, I mean. My mother has told me that you've read some of her letters at the Women's Missionary Union meetings. I think that's really good of you. I'd . . . I'd like to hear one, too."

Mollie just stared at the young man across the counter. He really *was* good-looking. Sandy brown hair, a little tousled, framed hazel eyes, and a slightly lopsided grin. Two years in college and he didn't look like a boy anymore.

"Uh, well . . . sure," she said. She hadn't spent this much time talking to George Meriweather in her whole life, even though they'd been in Sunbeam Band since she was six and he was ten. She leaned back against the stool and started at the beginning of Ida's letter. No other customers came in, so she even read the part she hadn't read yet before he showed up.

"Wow," he said when she finished. "Really makes you think, doesn't it? About how easy it is to be a Christian in this country—it's even kind of expected."

Mollie nodded. She wanted to say something grown-up and wise, but she was at a loss for words.

"Sounds like her asthma's doing better. Wasn't she back in Sha-Ling with her parents at the end of the letter?"

Mollie nodded again. *Speak, you silly!* she told herself.

"What did she mean asking if you'd found out about a nursing program yet? Is she coming back to America to go to college?" George asked.

Why did he keep talking about Ida! "I . . . I'm not

sure," Mollie stammered. "I'm trying to talk her into coming home. I think it would be really good for her. It's been tough on her, I think. Really sick a lot of the time . . . really lonely, too." And suddenly Mollie found herself talking about Ida, and how much she missed her, and how worried she'd been when Ida was so sick, and how hard it was to understand her life over there in China, and how scary and serious life on the mission field seemed to be.

Finally she ran out of words.

George's eyes softened. "She's lucky to have a friend like you." He absently picked up a penny whistle from a box sitting on the counter and seemed to study it. "And what about you. You have one more year at Hollins, right? Then what?"

"M-me? Well . . ." Would he laugh if she told him she wanted to study fashion design? "I'm going to apply to Albemarle Female College as soon as I get an appli—"

"In Charlottesville!" The hazel eyes crinkled in a grin. "That's where I'm going to school—at the University of Virginia. Say, I'll get you an application— one for Ida, too." He shrugged. "I have two more years—which means I'll still be there when you start Albemarle."

Mollie smiled weakly and watched George Meriweather walk toward the door, then turn back with a friendly wave. Then he was gone.

"I'll still be there when you start Albemarle. . . ."

That evening, she wrote a very long letter to Ida.

Chapter 10

The Climbing Tree

IDA'S EYES KEPT FLICKERING from the history text she was supposed to be reading to the college application that lay on the little table at her elbow. She gave up. Grabbing a fresh sheet of paper, she uncorked her ink bottle and dipped her pen.

Little Cross Roads, Tengchow
September 21, 1896

Dearest Mollie,
Thank you, thank you, thank you for sending me the application to Albemarle! Have you sent yours in yet? Oh, Mollie, I'm getting so excited that we might actually be together next year—at least in the same school. Do you know if nursing students have to room with other nursing

students? If not, please, please let's be roommates!

Your letter found me in Sha-Ling in August. Unfortunately, so did whatever sets off my asthma. Daddy thinks it might be the fields that surround Sha-Ling on every side—especially at harvest time when dust and pollen are in the air. I got by most of the summer months, but in August I had another severe asthma attack that put me in bed for almost a week! So I am back in Tengchow, where I fare a little better—maybe because it is near the sea??? Also, Dr. Randle keeps a close watch on me.

Mama tried to be brave, but I know she is upset that I could not stay in Sha-Ling. I think she is lonely, too. Also, she and Mrs. Chow are starting a school for girls this fall, and I wish I could help. Starting a school is hard. Many Chinese families don't think it's important for girls to be educated. They think the only thing girls are good for is to scrub and cook and fetch water, and then marry them off to the man who can pay the biggest bride price! Aunt Lottie says educating the girls and winning the families to Christ is the key.

If I didn't want to be a nurse, I might like to be a teacher. I'm not sure which is needed more here in China!

Speaking of education, Aunt Lottie is tutoring me so I don't fall behind in my schooling. Did you know she was the principal of a school in Georgia before she came to China? She knows Latin, French, and of course Chinese. She makes me read geography and history and botany—sometimes I think my eyeballs are going to fall out from so much reading! But if I do well in my exams this year, she said she would sign my college recommendation.

I haven't actually talked to my parents about going back to Virginia to attend college yet. Mama was upset *about me having to go back to Tengchow, so it wasn't the best time. Also, I overheard Daddy tell Mama that the mission board had to cut salaries this year. But my parents are coming to Tengchow for Christmas (so are the Pruitts!—can't wait to see Ashley and Little Ida) so I will talk to them then. Cross your fingers!*

"Ida? Have you finished your history reading yet?"

Ida jumped. "Um, not yet," she called back to the next room. Quickly she signed the letter, "Forever, your friend, Ida," and blotted the ink dry. But she frowned. Aunt Lottie's voice was hoarse most of the time now. She could only speak for short periods before losing it. But she kept on traveling, teaching the Bible, talking about Jesus. Not even Dr. Randle could get her to stop for long.

Ida sighed and opened her history text. On second thought she grabbed the letter again and added:

P.S. Did George Meriweather really like my little drawings? I can't believe you showed them to him! They're just doodles—nothing special.

P.P.S. I think he's sweet on you!

Christmas was especially festive at Little Cross Roads this year, with Pastor Baker and his wife, Nellie, coming from Sha-Ling to see Ida, as well as the four Pruitts from Hwanghsien. Miss Moon took advantage of the Bakers' and Pruitts' visit to take care of mission business during the month of January 1897, so Ida had a good long time to enjoy her "little sister" and "little brother." And the Chinese New Year came early—the new moon fell on February 1—so the two families decided to wait until after the celebrations to start back home.

Besides, the Pruitts wanted to consult with Dr. Randle about Ashley. The little boy wasn't exactly sick, but he got tired easily and always seemed to have a cold. Once again Dr. Randle gave the familiar diagnosis: low resistance. "He just doesn't have a good defense against sickness," the doctor told the Pruitts. "You must be especially careful that he isn't exposed to cholera or diphtheria or measles—he would have a hard time fighting them."

Today was the last Sunday in January, the day before the Year of the Rooster was ushered in with New Year's celebrations. Ida's parents and the Pruitts had gone visiting, and Ida had volunteered to look after the little boy while he napped. She settled herself at Lottie Moon's writing desk and started a letter to Mollie. But she'd only written a few paragraphs when eight-year-old Ida Pruitt came running into the sitting room, her hair ribbon flopping. "Ida! Ashley! Come out and play with us!"

Ida put a warning finger to her lips. Five-year-old Ashley, pale and thin, was asleep on some cushions.

"Well, he's asleep, so *you* come play!" begged the little girl. "Aunt Lottie said the Sunday school children could stay to play after lunch! You can teach them to jump rope!"

Ida shook her head wistfully. "I'm sorry, Little Ida. I . . . I can't jump rope anymore—I get all out of breath. Besides, I promised Ashley I'd sit with him. He's not feeling very well, you know."

Little Ida stamped her foot. "Ashley's no fun— he's always tired. And now you're no fun, either!" The little girl turned and stomped out of the room.

Ida's eyes felt hot with self-pity as she watched Little Ida run past the window along the veranda and out into the garden, bare now in winter's gray grip. But on this sunny winter Sunday, the children were in a festive mood and wanted to play, bundled up in their padded jackets. Often after church and Sunday school, Lottie Moon fed the children a simple lunch and let them play in her garden, a favorite play yard.

Still sitting at Lottie Moon's writing desk, Ida looked over at the sleeping boy. "Guess we're cousins under the skin, Ashley," she whispered. "Can't do this, can't do that, be careful, don't run . . . I'm sick of hearing it, too!"

She sighed. Picking up her pen, she dipped it once more into the bottle of ink to finish her letter.

. . . I finally talked to my parents about going to Albemarle. Now I have to face the hard truth: It's not going to happen—at least not this year. Aunt Lottie says I'm doing very well in my studies; that isn't the problem. But the mission board is trying to pay off a large debt, so all missionaries have had to take a cut in salary. No one is traveling home on furlough; no new

missionaries are coming to China right now. There just isn't any money!

Oh, Mollie, I'm so disappointed! I don't know how I can wait another whole year to see you. Now some other lucky girl will be your roommate at Albemarle. I think Mama's a little relieved; she worries too much about my health. But Aunt Lottie says God will provide . . . somehow. She is writing on my behalf to the mission board, telling them how badly nurses and doctors are—

Screams from the garden jolted Ida from the page she was writing. "Help! Aunt Lottie! Ida! Help! Help! Come quickly!"

Ida saw Lottie Moon running down the veranda from another part of the house. She ran to the doorway—and stopped. A cluster of frightened children stood in the garden beneath the chinaberry tree, staring at a crumpled figure on the ground. Miss Moon moved quickly and knelt down beside the child, who wasn't moving.

"He—he was climbing th-the tree, an' he just fell down!" cried Little Ida. The other children nodded in mute terror.

Ida stood frozen in the doorway. Who was it? Not Little Ida—thank God! It looked like Lin, one of the older boys, about eleven. How badly was he hurt?

Just then she felt a small form press close to her side. Ashley Pruitt's small face was chalk white. "Is Lin . . . dead?" he whispered.

"Ida!" Lottie Moon called over her shoulder as she

felt for the child's pulse. "Go get Dr. Randle! Quickly!"

Quickly? Oh, if she could only run without losing her breath! Grabbing a warm, padded jacket to put over her tunic and trousers, Ida told Ashley to "not move!" and dashed for the garden gate.

The boy was dead. Dr. Randle said it was a broken neck. He had fallen "just so." Miss Moon herself went with Dr. Randle to deliver the poor, lifeless body to his shocked and grieving mother. Lottie Moon still hadn't come home.

Ida lay propped on the kang in the room behind the kitchen in Little Cross Roads, with a hot, wet towel pressed to her chest, trying to ease the pain in her lungs after her mad dash to find Dr. Randle. Little Ida was curled in a corner of the kang, fast asleep, exhausted with shock and tears. Ashley cuddled against Ida, his thumb in his mouth, but his eyes were wide and thoughtful. As evening shadows filled the room, Ida could hear the low murmur of voices in the next room as her parents and the Pruitts discussed the tragic accident.

"Ida, what is heaven like?"

The question startled Ida. Ashley was looking up at her with his big eyes. "Heaven? Why . . . uh, I don't really know, Ashley. I know it's nice."

"How do you know?"

"Um, because Jesus is there mostly. There's no crying or sickness . . . no sin or sadness . . ." Ida's

mind raced, trying to remember what her father had preached about heaven.

Whack! Whack! Whack!

Ida sat up. What was that sound? She could hear chairs scraping and footsteps in the next room. The grown-ups must have heard it, too.

Whack! Whack! Whack!

Ashley scooted off the kang and ran into the next room. Ida laid aside the wet towel and followed, hugging her wrapper around her.

Whack! Whack! The strange sound continued. As Ida and Ashley got to the doorway, at first all she could see were her parents and the Pruitts standing outside in the lamplight from the windows. Then Ida saw what was making that sound.

Lottie Moon was chopping down the chinaberry tree.

Mollie looked up from Ida's letter. Trees all over the campus of Hollins Institute were covered with the fresh green fuzz of spring. The bench under the old oak tree was dappled in sunlight sifting through the budding branches. She looked at the date on the letter again—Ida must have mailed it right after the Chinese New Year, in early February. Now it was early April, and graduation was right around the corner.

But Ida would not be coming home. They wouldn't be going to Albemarle together next fall.

Mollie felt like ripping the letter up and throwing away the pieces! It was just so unfair! Didn't God know how much Mollie wanted Ida to come home? Ida was her *friend* . . . her very best friend ever. Oh, she'd had a lot of friends at Hollins. But not a friend like Ida. Not really. Ida always stuck with her, no matter what. Always listened to her ideas. Always had something encouraging to say when Mollie was feeling blue. Was always there for her . . . except not now. Not for the past three and a half years. Ida was in China, and maybe she'd be stuck there *forever*.

Mollie sighed and looked back at the letter. Guess she should finish it. Ida was writing about Lottie Moon taking an ax to the tree. Mollie snorted. *That* would have been something to see.

 . . . There's a big, gaping hole in the garden where the chinaberry tree stood. The garden looks ugly and empty now. Mama said Aunt Lottie doesn't want to be reminded of what happened, that's why she cut it down. But I think she cut it down because she would rather get rid of her chinaberry tree than have one more child hurt climbing it. That's just the way she is.

Lin's death has affected Ashley in a strange way. He keeps asking people about heaven. Little Ida thinks he's just being a pest. But I wonder. He's had so much sickness himself. Does he think about heaven a lot?

Maybe because Ashley's been asking so many questions about heaven, Aunt Lottie gathered all the Sunday school children together and let them ask questions about Lin's death. She didn't brush them off or say, "You're too young to understand." Aunt Lottie says Lin was sometimes a little scamp, but he loved Jesus and was very faithful about coming to Sunday school. She assured the children that he's in heaven, and that we'll see him again. I watched Ashley's face. He smiled. Now he can imagine someone he knows in *heaven; maybe that makes it more real for him.*

Then Aunt Lottie told the children that none of us knows how long we have to live on this earth. That's why it's important to make our lives count for God, even when we're young. She told the story of the boy who gave his lunch of five small loaves of bread and two fish to Jesus—and Jesus fed five thousand people with it! All the boy had was his lunch, but he let Jesus use it.

Oh, Mollie, I want my life to count for God, too! But just when I think I might be able to do something for God—like help Mama with the new girls school in Sha-Ling—this mean old asthma trips me up. I'm really sick of it!

"Mollie! Come on! Mrs. Pendergrass gave us permission to walk to town. Want to come?" Evangeline was dancing on the lawn like a sunbeam skipping on the surface of a pond. The other girls—Sarah, Laura, and Celia—were laughing and chasing one another around the bushes like springtime colts, happy to be outside without their coats.

Mollie shook her head and waved them on. Her spirit was unsettled. Had she ever done anything that would "count for God"? Besides collecting eggs from Chicken Lottie and China Moon and giving the egg money to missions, that is. And even then, she gave the least amount she could—one tenth, a tithe.

Mollie suddenly jumped up from the bench and started to run, blinking back the tears spilling onto her cheeks. The boy who gave his lunch . . . five thousand people fed . . . Ida putting all her "dress" money into the mission offering . . . missionaries who had to cut their salaries ... Ida unable to study nursing because there wasn't any money ...

Something was wrong. Very, very wrong.

Chapter 11

End of a Dream?

I DA WATCHED MRS. CHOW deftly fold the wonton dough over the little mound of cooked pork and finely chopped vegetables and slide it into the pot of simmering chicken broth. Under Mrs. Chow's eagle eye, Ida carefully rolled up the next wonton and slid it into the soup, then started on another.

The moist air in the little kitchen of the Sha-Ling mission house was comforting to Ida's lungs, and she was enjoying the cooking lesson. Young Pastor Li from P'ingtu was coming for his monthly study time with Pastor Baker, and Ida and Mrs. Chow were cooking up a special meal for their guest. Somewhere out on the street she could hear the *ting-a-ling* of a peddler's cart as she plopped the pork-and-vegetable mixture on another square of dough and folded the four corners.

Ting-a-ling! Ting-a-ling!

Ida looked up. That wasn't a peddler's cart. That was the garden gate! Oh no. How long had their guest been standing there? Wiping her hands on her apron, which she was wearing over her everyday tunic and trousers, she headed for the door.

"Come back here, young missy!" scolded Mrs. Chow. "You can't be running out into the cold air. I will go."

But Ida ignored her. She was tired of being treated like an invalid. She was perfectly capable of going to the garden gate like anyone else. But she shrugged her arms into her padded coat before heading across the small garden to the gate.

"Pastor Li!" she said happily, greeting the young Chinese man with her hands pressed together and a slight bow. "*Ni hao!* Hello! Come in." And then she realized he was not alone. The other man was English, with slicked hair and a thin moustache—

"Dr. Randle!" Ida exclaimed. "I didn't know you were coming, too. Oh, this will be jolly fun."

"Aha," said Dr. Randle. "Now you're making fun of me. 'Jolly' indeed."

It was a joke they batted back and forth like a badminton cock. Lottie Moon had picked up Dr. Randle's English expression until everything was "jolly" this or that. Then Ida teased them both by using it, too.

"I was visiting some patients in P'ingtu," the doctor explained as they entered the warm kitchen and shut out winter's chill. "When I discovered Pastor Li was coming to visit your father, I decided this was as good a time as any to check how my favorite patient is doing in Sha-Ling this year."

Ida gave him a fleeting smile and a small shrug. What was there to say? It was good to be home with her mother and father. Some days she was able to help with the girls school, which was in its second year; other days she had to rest a lot. But at least she'd been able to stay in Sha-Ling past her seventeenth birthday, past harvest time, past Christmas . . .

As 1898 unfolded into the Chinese Year of the Dog, she tried to keep busy and not think too much about missing her first year in Albemarle's nursing program. Mollie was already in her second term of the first year. Well, it would just take Ida a little longer.

"Pastor Li! . . . and Dr. Randle! This is a surprise!" Ida's parents arrived on the heels of their guests, letting Ida off the hook. She busied herself helping Mrs. Chow serve the festive supper of wonton soup, fried rice sticks with shrimp and cabbage, orange tapioca pudding, and tea, and the conversation around the small table was lively.

"God is doing a mighty work in P'ingtu through this young man," said Dr. Randle, fire dancing in his eyes. "I saw it for myself! The church in P'ingtu is adding new believers every week! Thomas, we need more Chinese preachers like this young man."

Pastor Li bowed his head humbly. "But it was La

Di Mu who first told me about Jesus . . . and Pastor Baker who walks me deep into the Scripture."

"Yes, yes," said Dr. Randle. "But when the people hear the Gospel from one of their own, they cannot dismiss it as a 'foreign religion.' I tell you, Thomas, the man is an evangelist! Hundreds are hearing the Word and becoming Christians."

Ida knew her father enjoyed his study times with Li Show-Ting, who had been a Confucian scholar before he became a Christian. The young man was educated, thoughtful, even brilliant. After supper, the two excused themselves and disappeared into the small storage room that Pastor Baker used as a study, leaving Nellie Baker and Ida with Dr. Randle. Mrs. Chow had already gone home to her own family.

Dr. Randle fixed Ida with his calm, dark eyes. "Your mother tells me that you are still determined to go back to Virginia and begin a nursing program as soon as the money is available."

"Oh yes!" Ida was excited to talk about it. "I . . . it's hard to wait, especially since China needs doctors and nurses so badly. Well . . . *you* know that." She reddened. "But I'm trying to be patient."

To her discomfort, Dr. Randle didn't respond immediately but just nodded thoughtfully. What was he thinking? Did he think she wasn't smart enough? But Aunt Lottie said her marks were excellent.

"Ida," he said finally, "we need to talk frankly. Your asthma limits you severely. You are managing well—but just managing. As your doctor, I need to be honest. You simply do not have the physical stamina to handle the demands of nursing. *Especially* in China, where nurses and doctors are stretched so thin and must travel from village to village, from mission to mission, and are exposed to all sorts of diseases. No, no. You must seriously consider another program of study—maybe teaching. By correspondence course if possible."

Ida just stared at the doctor, stunned. She looked at her mother's face, aching with tender concern— but she could tell her mother agreed with Dr. Randle.

Ting-a-ling! Ting-a-ling! The bell on the garden gate rang insistently, even though the hour was late. Ida felt like screaming, *Go away! I don't want any more visitors right now!* But her mother went out, and in a moment she came back with a wiry man who looked vaguely familiar to Ida. The man was breathing heavily and looked dog-tired.

"Doctor must come quickly! All missionaries in Hwanghsien bad sick. Pruitt boy—can't breathe, heart go funny. Must come quickly. Now!"

Alarm crowded out Ida's own shock and hurt. That's where she had seen the man—at the Hwanghsien mission. But Hwanghsien was three days away! Could Dr. Randle get there in time?

Albemarle Female Institute nestled grandly among the tree-lined streets of Charlottesville, Virginia. Once more spring had come to Virginia with a sweetness that Mollie was sure existed nowhere else on earth.

The thought surprised her. She who had grown up dreaming of travels to new and exotic countries was sitting here on a plain wooden bench on the front commons of Albemarle, drinking in the fragrant air and sunshine as if she couldn't get enough of it.

"What did you want to tell me, Mollie?" The young man sitting next to her looked anxious. "You *are* coming to my graduation in June, aren't you?"

She looked at him as though suddenly remembering that he was there. "Of course, George! I'm happy for you—though it's going to be lonely at Albemarle next year without you in town."

George Meriweather nodded, still looking miserable. "But maybe Ida Baker will be here by then—you'd like that, I know."

Sudden tears blurred Mollie's vision. She swallowed. "That's—that's what I wanted to tell you, George. Here. Read this letter." Mollie handed the young man several pages of folded stationery.

Cautiously, George took the fragile pages with the flowing script.

Sha-Ling, China
March 15, 1898

Dearest friend,

Oh, Mollie, can you help me bear it? My heart is so sore, I want to rip it out and throw it away. I've cried so many tears, I have no more left to cry.

Little Ashley Pruitt died two weeks ago of diptheria—two hours before Dr. Randle was able to get

134

to his bedside. Why, oh why, did God take him? Tell me! Ashley was too sick to travel, so they had to send a messenger—three days on the road from Hwanghsien to Sha-Ling, then three days back with the doctor. Six precious days. But it was too late.

Oh, Mollie, if ever I wondered if I should become a nurse—only one nurse, I know, but here in China, one person can make such a difference! Look at Pastor Li! He listened in the shadows when Lottie Moon was sharing with the women of P'ingtu, then came to her privately to hear more about Jesus. Now he has become an evangelist, and hundreds are turning to Jesus! But it started with one missionary who told one Chinese. . . .

I have so little to give to God, but I wanted to give it! I wanted to be a nurse. Couldn't God have used me, like He used the boy who gave his lunch of five loaves and two fish? But even that has been snatched from me. Dr. Randle says my asthma—

"Oh no," murmured George. He quickly finished the letter, then folded it gently. "I . . . I don't know what to say. She—"

"Don't." Mollie put up a hand. "Don't say anything. But I want you to come with me while I do something. I need . . . a friend, to give me courage."

Looking puzzled and a little alarmed, George followed Mollie up the campus walk toward the administration building of the women's college. He hesitated at the door, but she rolled her eyes. "Men are allowed in the *administration* building, goose."

He grinned, glad for the break in the tension, and followed her into the office marked *Registrar*.

"Can I help you—Miss Jones, isn't it?" said the thin woman behind the desk, small spectacles balanced on her nose.

"Yes. Mollie Jones . . . I'm a first-year student." Mollie took a deep breath, looked at George, then back to the desk. "I'd like to change my program of study."

✧ ✧ ✧ ✧

Shouts and hoofbeats woke Ida from a sound sleep. Anguished voices outside cried in Chinese, "Stop! Help!" followed by screams of pain.

Instantly awake, her heart pumping wildly, Ida scrambled off the kang, unlatched the wooden shutters, and opened them a crack. All she could see was the dancing light of half a dozen torches and a blur of bodies and horses flying past.

"Ida, get back!" ordered her father. Thomas Baker came into the dark room, with Li Show-Ting at his heels. The P'ingtu pastor had come for his monthly study time and had been asleep on a mat in the Bakers' kitchen. Ida backed away from the window as her father opened the shutters a little wider and peered out.

"Li! What is happening?—oh, God, have mercy! I recognize Chang and Ti-Pin, two of our Christian men! And . . . there are others!"

Ida caught a glimpse of soldiers on horseback and men on foot running alongside—tied by their long pigtails to the saddle horns! As she watched, one man stumbled and fell and was dragged out of sight by his hair. Ida's fist went to her mouth in shock.

"Boxers," breathed Pastor Li, crowding close to the window. He turned to Ida's father. "We must go to P'ingtu at first light—that's where these soldiers are heading with their prisoners. I will send word to La Di Mu. She is experienced in dealing with the government. She will know what we must do."

❖ ❖ ❖

The two men decided that Ida and her mother should not be left alone in Sha-Ling. But the short journey from Sha-Ling to P'ingtu by oxcart was filled with anxiety. Were the Boxers harassing only Chinese Christians? Or missionaries, too? Pastor Li persuaded Nellie Baker to shed her American dress and wear the loose-fitting tunic and trousers her husband and daughter had already adopted, so as not to attract attention.

But the flight to P'ingtu was nothing compared to the frustration of waiting at Pastor Li's house one day, two . . . then a whole week. Ida heard her father and Pastor Li arguing back and forth about who should go speak on behalf of the Chinese Christians who had been thrown in jail.

"You can't go, Li!" Thomas Baker protested. "If they capture you, they have snatched the shepherd of the sheep. I will go. There is a treaty that protects Americans—"

"The Boxers care nothing for treaties!" Li Show-Ting scoffed. "They hate all foreigners—but especially missionaries. You have a wife and daughter to care for. No! We need help from the Baptist mission."

Yes, they decided, they would wait for Lottie Moon's reply. The senior missionary had many connections in Shantung Province and was well respected. But the worry remained. Had Lottie Moon even gotten Pastor Li's message?

Ida tried to be brave, but her spirit felt fragile.

Her heart had not yet mended from Ashley Pruitt's death—and Dr. Randle's medical verdict had snatched her dream of becoming a nurse and dashed it into a thousand pieces. And now . . . now they had left everything behind in Sha-Ling except for a few clothes. Her life was being scattered in all directions, like dandelion fluff blown about by the wind.

Each evening she peeked from Pastor's Li's windows, searching for the moon. Was Mollie looking, too? She couldn't write—and no letters would find her here. The China moon was her only connection. . . .

Bored, Ida spent many hours just watching passersby. Pastor Li's house was right on the street—no walled garden—and at first Ida didn't pay any attention to the official-looking covered sedan chair that came by one late afternoon—until the bearers set it down in front of the house. The front curtains of the chair were open, and inside sat a pompous-looking man in a silk robe and short coat. He wore big, round glasses and a cap with the bright red button of a government officer. To Ida's surprise, the official got out of the chair and walked up to Pastor Li's door, arms held formally across his middle, hidden inside big, wide sleeves.

"Daddy! Pastor Li!" she whispered frantically. "A man—somebody important is coming!"

Alarmed, Pastor Li sprang to the window. "No soldiers. It may be a trick . . . but I must open the door."

Silently, the Baker family stood together as Pastor Li greeted the official with a bow and invited him in. But once the door had closed behind him, the stranger took off his hat and his glasses and broke out into a wide grin. "Don't you recognize me, Li Show-Ting?" said a familiar throaty voice.

The Bakers and Pastor Li gasped. It was Lottie Moon!

Lottie Moon had been warned by other missionaries in Tengchow not to attempt the trip to P'ingtu. Bands of angry Boxers were roaming the roads, armed with orders from the Empress Dowager that missionaries and Christians were not protected. She had decided the only way to travel safely was to travel boldly and openly—but in disguise.

"But could I rest if I did not try to support my spiritual children here in P'ingtu when they are suffering?" she said simply to the Bakers and Pastor Li.

Discarding her disguise, but dressed in her own Chinese clothes, Lottie Moon and the two pastors all went together the next day to learn the fate of the jailed Christians. Ida and her mother waited anxiously all day and breathed a prayer of relief when they returned many hours later. The news was good and bad. The thirteen prisoners had been released by the time they got there, but they had been badly beaten and tortured.

That evening a delegation of P'ingtu church members came secretly to Pastor Li's house, arriving one by one so as not to attract attention. Tears flowed as they thanked Lottie Moon for risking her own life to come to them.

"But it is a very serious time," said one of the church elders gravely. "Your presence may cause more harm than good. The Boxers are becoming very bold. No Christian is safe—especially those who associate with foreign missionaries. We have come . . ." The older man swallowed hard, and his chin quivered. "We have come to ask you to leave—leave China! For your own safety. And ours."

Ida could not believe what she was hearing. Leave China? Surely Lottie Moon would never agree to that. She was not one to run from danger.

But to Ida's surprise Lottie Moon nodded slowly. "I fear you are right, wise uncle. The American consul has been begging the missionaries in Tengchow to leave China immediately and go to Japan. I would not listen. I do not fear for my own safety. But . . ." She looked at the Baker family, who were gaping at her, openmouthed. "If our presence puts our Chinese brothers and sisters in danger, then we must leave."

Ida's head was spinning. Japan? *Japan?* No! She'd been ripped from her home once. But China was home now! She didn't want to be ripped from her home once more.

Leaning into her father's arms, she began to cry—loud, pent-up sobs that came from pain deep within. The last fragment of Ida's dream had just been crushed into dust.

Chapter 12

A Nurse for China

Twenty-year-old Ida Baker stood on the deck of the Chinese gunboat *Hai-Chai* as it nosed its way into Tengchow harbor. She turned and waved at Mr. Sah, the captain, in the wheelhouse—the same captain who had welcomed the missionaries on board when they had been ordered out of the province two years earlier. Mr. Sah, a Christian, had given them his best cabins and served them wonderful meals in spite of the grumblings of some of his crew who were sympathetic to the Boxer Rebellion. Then he transferred them safely to the American warship, the *Yorktown*, which had delivered the missionaries to safety in Japan.

142

Two years in Japan . . . Ida could hardly believe it. At first, like all the other missionaries, she had felt displaced, awkward, useless. Even a missionary as skilled and useful as Lottie Moon was like a fish out of water. None of them could speak Japanese— not even Miss Moon. They didn't know anyone. Where should they go? What would they do? What *could* they do?

A Southern Baptist missionary family in Japan, the McCollums, invited the displaced missionaries to their mission house in Fukuoka for a visit. Both Miss Moon and Ida were delighted by the large brood of McCollum children. "Oh, you've got your quiver full," Lottie teased her new friends over tea.

"Yes, and we thank God for every one," sighed Mrs. McCollum. "But they keep me so busy that I don't have time to go visiting, taking the Gospel to the women in the surrounding villages like you did, Miss Moon. I envy your freedom."

Ida saw a light go on in Aunt Lottie's eyes. "Hmm. We can either be frogs at the bottom of a well, or . . ."

Ida and her mother and Mrs. McCollum all looked at Lottie Moon strangely. Frogs?

Miss Moon laughed. "A wise Chinese saying—'A frog at the bottom of a well has a limited view of the sky.'"

Still they looked confused.

"See here," she said. "There's more than one way to do things if we get out of the well and get a bigger perspective! Mrs. McCollum, you speak fluent Japanese but can't go visiting. I don't speak a word of

Japanese, but I love children. What if we switch roles? I'll take care of your children when you want to go visiting. Ida will help me, won't you, Ida?"

Amazed, Ida nodded eagerly. The McCollums' big family reminded her of Mollie's lively household back in Sugar Grove, and how dearly she loved spending time there.

With Miss Moon's wise encouragement, all the missionaries found things they could do in Japan— teaching English, freeing up the Japanese missionaries by taking on household work or writing letters. It was true—the sky was bigger than they expected. And Ida found that rocking the McCollum baby, combing the little girls' hair, teaching them to draw and practice their letters, and reading stories helped heal, little by little, the ache left by Ashley Pruitt's death.

But her asthma stayed about the same. Sometimes she felt almost normal—as long as she didn't do any hard physical activity like running or scrubbing floors. Other times the pain in her lungs tightened until she could hardly breathe, and she coughed and wheezed for days. At those times she felt exactly like the frog at the bottom of the well. Would her asthma *always* limit her view of the sky?

Finally, in 1901, the American consul in Chefoo sent word that the Boxer Rebellion had fizzled out and that it was safe to return.

Now, as she stood on the deck of the *Hai-Chai*, Ida watched Tengchow rise up on the shoreline and the curved roofs of the Eight Immortals Pavilion take shape. The gunboat threaded its way through fishing boats and sampans selling silk cloth, necklaces of jade or pearls, or baskets of fresh fish.

Ida had no idea what the future held, but . . . it was good to be home.

The Boxers had destroyed or damaged a lot of the mission property in Tengchow, Hwanghsien, P'ingtu, and Sha-Ling. Many of the Chinese Christians had been chased from their homes, beaten, or jailed. Some had even died rather than give up their belief in Jesus.

"That is something to thank God for, not despair," said Lottie Moon firmly as the missionaries met in Tengchow to regroup. "Their faith endured, even in persecution. The blood of martyrs is always precious seed that falls into the ground, and dies, and brings forth fruit."

"The Chinese government is offering to pay for the damages to our property," said Ida's father.

"No," said Miss Moon firmly. "We will take no payment unless it is offered by the people who actually did the damage as a sign of their repentance."

The missionaries were surprised. But they saw the wisdom of Miss Moon's decision in the next few weeks and months. The bell on the gate of Little Cross Roads rang constantly as more and more Chinese men and women came to the Tengchow mission, wanting to know more about "the Jesus way."

Curiosity got the better of Ida's father one day, when a well-to-do businessman in Tengchow brought his wife and three beautifully dressed children to Little Cross Roads. "Why do you ask about the Jesus way?" Thomas Baker asked them bluntly.

The man gave a little bow. "We always thought you Americans just wanted to take money from the pockets of Chinese. We thought you would demand big payment for damage to your property—it would be your legal right. We were wrong. But . . . if you don't want money, why are you here?"

A big grin spread over Thomas Baker's face. "To tell you the Good News!"

Hundreds of new believers were baptized in Tengchow—and the damaged property hadn't even been repaired yet. The missionaries were excited. God was building the *real* church in China!

Ida was left behind when her parents returned to Sha-Ling until the mission house could be repaired. With everyone feeling so positive about the new opportunities for mission work in China, Ida felt selfish about the disappointment that gnawed away at her: There had been no letters waiting for her when she returned to Tengchow. But why? Had Mollie forgotten about her? She had written to Mollie from Japan, trying to tell her that they had left China. Had her letters even reached Albemarle? Maybe Mollie wasn't even at the college anymore! Had someone seen her talent in clothing design and given her a scholarship to Paris or London or. . . ?

One day, weak from a recent bout of asthma, she

sat on the stump of the old chinaberry tree, watching Aunt Lottie weeding her flower garden. Suddenly tears of loneliness and self-pity slid down her cheeks, giving away her secret.

"What is it, child?" Lottie Moon's voice was kind.

Ida found herself pouring out her disappointments—losing track of her best friend, the end of her dream of becoming a nurse, her feelings of uselessness. "Why did God bring me to China, Aunt Lottie? *Why?*"

To Ida's surprise, Aunt Lottie didn't give her a little spiritual pep talk. She just looked at Ida thoughtfully for a few moments and then said, "Some new missionaries are arriving in Tengchow next week. I would like you to help me prepare a welcome for them."

Ida sighed. Yes, she supposed she could do that. Not that Aunt Lottie really *needed* her help. She was just trying to make her feel useful. Well, it was better than nothing.

But even as she chopped vegetables and dusted furniture and prepared the guest bedrooms with cut flowers from the garden, Ida's spirit felt like a lead weight in the pit of her stomach. Her thoughts were jumbled prayers. *Oh, God, I just wanted you to use me. Don't you need a nurse here in China? Couldn't you use me?*

A messenger brought word that the new missionaries had arrived by ship in Chefoo and were coming overland by shentze to Tengchow. Ida tried to help with the last-minute cleaning, but another attack of asthma put her in bed, wheezing and coughing, and Aunt Lottie had to finish dusting the furniture and making up the kangs with freshly washed quilts.

From her sleeping kang, propped on pillows so she could breathe more easily, Ida heard the bell jangling on the garden gate. Soon she heard Aunt Lottie's warm, welcoming voice, and the light voices of strangers. Americans. With Virginia accents. With a groan she turned her face to the wall. The arrival of new missionaries just made her feel more of a failure. She hoped Aunt Lottie would not try to introduce her.

But she heard the curtain in the doorway rustle and someone come into the little room. She kept her eyes closed; maybe Aunt Lottie would think she was asleep. But then she heard her name.

"Ida?"

Ida's eyes flew open. That wasn't Aunt Lottie's voice. But it was familiar—

Her hand flew to the locket she wore around her neck as she rolled over and stared at her visitor. Unruly corkscrews of straw-colored hair escaped the twist at the back of the young woman's head. A hint of freckles sprinkled over her nose beneath laughing green eyes.

"Mollie!" Ida gasped. "You . . . *you?"*

"Oh, dear Ida . . . didn't you get my letters? Didn't you know I was coming?"

Ida sucked hard, trying to catch her breath. All she could do was shake her head and hold out her

arms. Mollie crawled onto the kang and threw herself into Ida's arms. Together they laughed and cried and hugged and looked at each other and hugged some more.

The two young women finally wiped their eyes and blew their noses as Lottie Moon came into the tiny room with a tray of hot tea. Mollie did most of the talking, laughing and rolling her eyes as she described the journey by shentze from Chefoo. "It was just like you described it in your letters, Ida! Rougher than a storm at sea."

Lottie Moon poured more tea. "Ida thinks she's

useless to God here in China," she said casually. "What do you think, Mollie?"

Ida's cheeks burned. Aunt Lottie didn't have to rub it in.

But to her surprise, Mollie's eyes filled with tears. "Oh, Ida. Didn't you say China needed nurses and doctors? God has used *you* to bring a nurse to China!"

Ida stared. "Y-you? A nurse?"

Mollie nodded.

"But—but what happened to studying clothing design, and—and going to Paris, and—"

Mollie shrugged. "I couldn't. I couldn't just keep doing what *I* wanted to do, not when all your letters spilled over with China's great need for missionaries . . . your letters *and* all the letters Miss Moon kept writing to the Women's Missionary Union, harping on the same chord." She rolled her eyes in her old, familiar way and grinned, then grew serious again. "Oh, Ida, I admired your decision to become a nurse—I was even jealous, because you had such a clear *purpose* for your life. But your letters also made me feel more and more selfish. There I was, fussing about sleeve fashions and petticoats and the latest dress length, and here *you* were wearing baggy Chinese pajamas—"

Ida pulled at her rumpled Chinese tunic. "These are *not* pajamas," she protested. She heard Aunt Lottie chuckle.

But Mollie ignored her. "You really made me think about what it meant to 'give my life to Jesus.' Was *I* willing to give myself to Jesus—like the boy who gave his five loaves and two fish—and let Him use me?"

"Oh, Mollie, I didn't mean to—"

"Hush, Ida Baker. I know you didn't mean to do anything. You were just being you! But God was using you to soften up my stubborn old heart. And when your little Ashley died because the doctor arrived too late . . . and when you got sick and couldn't follow your dream of becoming a nurse for China . . . suddenly I knew what God wanted me to do!" Mollie grinned widely. "Here I am, Ida Baker, and it's all your fault!"

Lottie Moon picked up the tray of tea things. "And a certain new missionary nurse is going to need a tutor to teach her Chinese, and *I* can't take time from my work right now. I need an assistant, someone fluent in English and Chinese . . . hmm, someone like you, Ida." She winked at Ida and swept out of the room. "It's getting late. Supper will be ready in about half an hour," she called back over her shoulder.

Mollie wrinkled her forehead and looked anxiously at Ida. "Supper? Not . . . sea worms, I hope."

In spite of herself, Ida started to laugh. She coughed and sputtered, and finally found her voice. "No, we spared you. Just chicken and noodles." Suddenly Ida's face sobered. "Speaking of chicken . . . whatever happened to Chicken Lottie and China Moon?"

"Um, they got old and stopped laying. . . ."

Ida made a face. "Stew?"

Mollie nodded guiltily. "It was good, though—Oh, Ida, look!"

Ida looked to the open window where Mollie was pointing. Twilight had crept unnoticed into Aunt Lottie's garden, and a full moon was rising above the garden wall, hanging golden and round in a velvet China sky.

She reached out for Mollie's hand, and the two young women huddled close, watching the moon rise. A deep peace settled over Ida's whole being, soothing the rawness in her chest and in her spirit. God was working His purpose out and had drawn the two friends together again . . . drawn by a China moon.

More About Lottie Moon

LOTTIE MOON WAS BORN IN 1840, third in a family of
five girls and two boys, on the family's fifteen-
hundred-acre tobacco plantation known as
Viewmont. Her father, Edward Moon, was the larg-
est slaveholder (fifty-two slaves) in Albemarle
County; he was also a merchant and a lay leader in
the Baptist church. But Lottie was only thirteen
when her father died in a riverboat accident.

The Moon family valued education, and at age
fourteen Lottie went to school at the Virginia Female Seminary (similar to high school) and later the
Albemarle Female Institute, where she earned both
her bachelor's and Master of Arts degree in teaching.
A spirited and outspoken girl, Lottie was indifferent
to her Southern Baptist upbringing until her late

teens, when God touched her heart during a spiritual revival at Albemarle.

There were precious few opportunities for educated females in the mid-1800s, though her older sister Orianna became a physician and served as a Confederate doctor during the Civil War. Lottie helped her mother maintain Viewmont during the war, once hiding the family silver in a field from approaching Union soldiers, but when the threat evaporated, she was unable to find it again.

After the Civil War, Lottie taught at female academies first in Danville, Kentucky, and later helped set up Cartersville Female High School in Georgia. The school was thriving academically (though not financially) under her leadership as associate principal when she felt a quite different call: to go to China as a missionary.

Single women on the mission field? Most mission work at that time was done by married men. But the wives of China missionaries T. P. Crawford and Landrum Holmes had discovered an important reality: Only women could reach Chinese women, and they needed help. To everyone's surprise, Lottie's younger sister Edmonia accepted a call to go to North China in 1872. Lottie followed a year later. She was thirty-three years old.

Edmonia didn't last as a missionary, but Lottie did. She was a petite woman, only four foot three, but she had stamina, a lively spirit, vision, and a passion to win souls for God. Mission policies of the time limited what ministry women could do. But

Lottie waged a slow, respectful, but relentless campaign to give women missionaries the freedom to minister and have an equal voice in mission proceedings. A prolific writer, she corresponded frequently with H. A. Tupper, head of the Southern Baptist Foreign Mission Board, informing him of the realities of mission work and the desperate need for more workers—women and men. She encouraged Southern Baptist women to organize mission societies in the local churches to help support additional missionary candidates—and to consider coming themselves. Many of her letters appeared as articles in denominational publications.

Catching her vision, Southern Baptist women organized Women's Missionary Unions (WMU) and even Sunbeam Bands for children to promote missions and collect funds to support missions. The first "Christmas Offering for Missions" in 1888 collected over three thousand dollars, enough to send three new missionaries to China.

Raised in a family "of culture and means," Lottie at first thought of the Chinese as an inferior people and insisted on wearing American clothes to maintain a degree of distance from these "heathen" people. But gradually she came to realize that the more she shed her westernized trappings and identified with the Chinese people, the more their simple curiosity about foreigners (and sometimes rejection) turned into genuine interest in the Gospel. She began wearing Chinese clothes, adopted Chinese customs, learned to be sensitive to and even admire Chinese culture and learning. In turn she was deeply loved and revered by the Chinese people.

Lottie began her tenure as a missionary by teaching in a girls school. But while accompanying some of the seasoned married women on "country visits" from village to village outside the bigger cities, she discovered her passion: direct evangelism. But there were so many hungry, lost souls, and so few missionaries! For forty years she kept up her not-so-gentle pressure for the Southern Baptists to become giving, sending, missions-minded people.

Lottie's home base as a missionary was Tengchow (today Penglai) in Shantung Province in North China. T. P. Crawford was the senior missionary there, but he had a reputation among both missionaries and the Chinese as an inflexible, contentious personality. Lottie often functioned as a peacemaker, able to see both sides of a dispute. She had her own strong opinions about different things, but she always worked respectfully *with* the Foreign Mission Board and with her fellow missionaries. Eventually Crawford resigned from the Mission and formed the independent Gospel Mission, taking several Southern Baptist missionaries with him. After Crawford's death, however, Lottie encouraged the board to receive the remaining GM missionaries "back into the fold."

Lottie extended her work into the interior, especially P'ingtu and Hwangshien, until additional missionaries arrived to carry on the work. Only then did she allow herself to take a much-needed furlough, the first in 1891, and the second in 1902. Lottie was very concerned that her fellow missionaries were burning out from lack of rest and renewal. The mindset back home was "go to the mission field, die on the mission field." Many never expected to see their friends and families again. Lottie argued that regular furloughs every ten years would literally extend the lives and effectiveness of seasoned missionaries. (Today most missionaries take a furlough roughly every four years.) She also took a month of rest each year.

The War with Japan (1894), the Boxer Rebellion (1900), and the Nationalist uprising (that overthrew the Qing Dynasty in 1911) all profoundly affected mission work. Famine and disease took their toll, as well. When Lottie returned from her second furlough in 1904, she agonized over the suffering of the people who were literally starving to death all around her. She pleaded for more money and more resources, but the mission board was heavily in debt and could send nothing. Mission salaries were voluntarily cut. Unknown to her fellow missionaries, Lottie Moon—the Southern belle who was once described as "over-indulged and under-disciplined"—shared her own meager money and food with anyone and everyone around her, severely affecting both her physical and mental health. In 1912, she weighed only fifty pounds. Alarmed, fellow missionaries arranged for her to be sent back home to the United States with a missionary companion, but she died on Christmas Eve on board ship in Kobe Harbor, Japan. Her body was cremated and the ashes were returned to loved ones in Virginia for burial.

Since her sacrificial death at the age of seventy-two, Lottie Moon has come to personify the missionary spirit for Southern Baptists and many other Christians, as well. The annual Lottie Moon Christmas Offering for Missions has raised a total of $1.5 billion for missions since 1888 and finances *half* the entire Southern Baptist missions budget every year.

For Further Reading

Allen, Catherine B. *The New Lottie Moon Story*. Nashville: Broadman Press, 1980. This excellent biography is out of print, but is available in many libraries or through interlibrary loans.

Rankin, Jerry. *A Journey of Faith and Sacrifice: Retracing the Steps of Lottie Moon*. Birmingham, Ala.: New Hope Publishers, 1996. Rankin retraced the missionary journeys of Lottie Moon, retelling her story and adding current reflections. Beautiful photographs of both China and Virginia, past and present, make this a "coffee table book" as well as a fascinating historical travelogue.